C000170811

On Scene and Dealing

The early career of DCI Sarah Rudd

by

Tony Drury

City Fiction

ISBN-13: 978-1-910040-07-2
ISBN-10: 1-910040-07-X

PROLOGUE: WHIPPED INTO SHAPE

October, 2002

She could feel her jeans being pulled down over her buttocks. Her knickers followed and the cold autumn air stung her exposed flesh. Her hands were tied together round the trunk of the oak tree. There was no other sound from the middle of the woods. She was shaking her head, trying to clear the effects of the Zolpidem that had been slipped into her drink.

'I'm a police officer,' she gasped.

'Aren't you the lucky one!' laughed her captor.

Detective Constable Sarah Rudd had already faced personal danger in her short career and her ability to think outside the box was contributing to her growing reputation. But this was different. This felt personal. Her mind was beginning to clear. She had been at the bar in the King George V pub with her pal, PC Rachel Grainger, where they had finally been able to laugh about the case of the disappearing cricket bat.

A blonde, tanned woman, at a nearby table, seemed to be trying to listen in on their conversation. Rachel had said she needed to go and meet her French suitor from the health club. Sarah had started to feel faint, and found herself being led outside to a car. Then she had lost consciousness.

'You stupid cow!' shouted her attacker. 'Think I'd let a Pom reject me?'

Sarah concentrated as never before. There would

be a weakness. This was a woman out of control: she'd make a mistake. Was this the person in the pub and why did her accent ring a bell?

She was shaken into consciousness by the crack of a whip.

'At home, my whip is twenty feet long. You're a lucky gal. This one fitted into my suitcase. Look at the leather cover on the handle.'

The woman thrust it into Sarah's face.

'When I start slicing your buttocks I need to make sure my grip is firm.' She laughed. 'Kangaroo hide, darlin'. See the strands and the knots at the end? They inflict the most pain. Might have been croc skin, but the bastard got away.'

The woman was working herself into a frenzy, which was not helped by Sarah's outward calm, which was beginning to annoy her.

'Time for a liquid laugh!' she shouted. She put the whip down and Sarah watched as she took a photograph out of her bag. The woman held it in front of her face. It showed the top of a blonde woman's head and a man's legs and penis. The woman was giving the man oral sex. From what Sarah could see it had been taken in a school classroom.

Realisation rushed in on Sarah. This was the Australian PE teacher from her husband's school: the one Nick had jokingly said he fancied. Imogen. But the vividness and intimacy were too much for Sarah. She was horribly sick down her front.

'He fancies me like ten sheep!' the Australian screamed. 'He wanted to fuck me, but he said he couldn't be unfaithful to you. He even stopped me sucking him.'

'Perhaps he realised you're an Australian whore!'

said Sarah.

'Oh, he was a true English gent; went on about loving you and apologised. He said he was sorry and that I'd got the wrong idea.'

She paused and wiped the spittle off her mouth.

'He didn't think about me, did he, Miss Perfect? Thought I was just an Aussie plaything.'

She picked up her weapon and rammed it into Sarah's face, cutting her cheek open with the wooden handle.

'You'll not be yabbering much more, honey.' Imogen spat on the ground. A gust of wind chilled Sarah's naked skin. 'Time for some pain. I'm going to give you eight lashes, which is one for each time your hubby told me he wanted to fuck me.'

She moved around and jerked Sarah's jeans and knickers down even further, feeling her buttocks. She then stood back, picked up the whip, attached the handle and cracked it. She pulled it back into the air.

Sarah exploded with anger and humiliation.

'Fuck you, Imogen! You know we'll get you.'

'Assuming you can find me,' she laughed.

'I promise you, whatever you do, it won't be enough. I'll track you down, wherever you are.'

Sarah was now struggling with the blood from her facial injury which was running down into her mouth.

'Big words, copper! Pity you're tied up.'

Again, she drew back the kangaroo hide weapon. As she went to lash her prisoner, she found that Sarah had broken free and was struggling to yank up her jeans.

'Don't they teach you knots in the Outback, Imogen?' she gasped.

The Australian charged with rage, landing on top

of Sarah. She started punching her face, but Sarah was strong. She managed to twist round and gain the upper hand, put her knee in her attacker's stomach and pinned her arms down. Then she grabbed the woman's hair and banged her head on the frozen ground. Imogen momentarily lost consciousness.

Sarah found that she was filled with hatred. She drew her fist back but then her training as DC Rudd took over.

'I'm arresting you for…'

She found that she was being lifted to her feet as officers from Stevenage Police arrived at the scene.

'Are you okay, Sarah?' asked DS Trimble. 'The medics are on their way.'

She struggled to adjust her jeans and cover up her embarrassment.

'I'm fine, Sarge. Fucking bitch!' she said, sinking to her knees. She was searching for a photograph.

As the Australian was led away, after being handcuffed and cautioned, Sarah allowed the medic to patch her up. Nick had now reached her and, while they drove home, explained that Rachel Grainger had been suspicious and had returned to the pub to discover that a drinker had seen Sarah being dragged to a car. She alerted the Sergeant on duty, who had phoned Nick, after putting out an 'attention to' message.

A police driver called in to report seeing a scuffle in a car park outside the Beacon Woods. He had thought it was a lovers' quarrel but had noted the registration number. The car had been stolen the day before from Stevenage High Street.

Nick did not know that, as they had walked away from the woods, Sarah had a photograph concealed in her pocket.

Over the next few days, the atmosphere between Sarah and her husband deteriorated until she started sleeping alone in the spare room. The tension exploded two days later when she was unable to conceal her anger.

Nick was sitting in the dining room marking examination papers when Sarah marched in and slammed the photograph down on the table.

'Your Australian whore claimed you did not have sex together!' she shouted.

'We never did, Sarah. You have my word on that.'

'No, she just sucked you off, you bastard!'

Nick picked up the photograph and examined it carefully.

'Oh my God!' he exclaimed.

A week later, on a Tuesday evening, Nick asked Sarah to sit down in their lounge, before leaving her alone. She became aware that a car had arrived and there was the sound of shutting doors. She remained tense and rigid.

Nick returned with a man of around fifty years of age.

'Sarah, this is James Cunniford. I teach his son at school.'

She looked at him in amazement. 'This can't be a police matter,' she said.

'Mrs Rudd, my wife and I simply want to apologise to you for any hurt that my family might have caused you.'

'What hurt?' shouted Sarah. She was confused. Nick left the room. A moment later, a smart teenager came in and stood in front of her.

'Sarah, this is Matthew Cunniford. He's here with

the permission of his parents.'

Sarah stared ahead of her. 'Nick, this is all wrong.'

'I'm the person in the photograph, Mrs Rudd.'

'With the Australian?' Sarah asked.

'Yes, I'm very sorry.'

Sarah looked at Nick and then at the pupil.

'It's your parents to whom you should apologise,' snarled Sarah.

Matthew was guided out of the room, and a few moments later, she heard a car drive away. Nick returned with a bunch of flowers. Sarah took them off him and threw them across the lounge. She checked Marcus's monitoring system: he was sleeping soundly.

'What a fucking charade, Nick!' she yelled. 'Do you think you can solve it like that?'

He remained silent, standing in front of his wife.

'You fucking wanted her, Nick!'

He said nothing.

'I accept she was attractive, but you shouldn't have flirted with her. You should have walked away.'

'You're still angry, aren't you, Sarah?' he said.

'Angry?' She grabbed him by the collar of his shirt. 'Angry?' she repeated. 'I'm torn apart with jealousy. I must know you want me in the same way.'

'That can never happen, Sarah.'

'There's no hope for us, Nick?'

'With Imogen, it was lust. Nothing more than that.'

'And with me?'

'You, Sarah, are simply one in a million. There is no man alive who could feel the way about you that I do.'

She released her grip and looked him in his face.

'And I can rely on that, Nick?'

'Yes, Sarah, you can. I made a terrible mistake with Imogen. In doing so, I found out what really matters to me.'

'Are you talking about Sarah Florence Rudd or Detective Constable Rudd?' she asked.

'Is there a difference?' he asked.

As they came together, Sarah sank her face into her husband's chest. It was a good question. Later that night, when she was clinging to his naked body, her mind went back to the start of it all.

To the day when PC Whitson first put on her uniform and walked straight into personal danger…

'YOU'RE NICKED!'

December, 1998

The blood looked so out of place, she almost didn't realise that's what it was until she saw the man and the knife. Then instinct and her training took over.

She was Sarah Florence Whitson... but not for much longer. She was PC 8377 Sarah Whitson, but she wasn't... yet. She was where she shouldn't have been, at a time when she should have been elsewhere. She thought she was in trouble with Inspector Renning Mantel, and she was right. Foolishly, she had accepted an invitation from Police Constable Irving Parlin, who was hoping to take her to bed... but he wouldn't.

***

Sarah had been the name of the midwife who had completed the home delivery twenty-eight years earlier. That she was named after the midwife summed up her mother, Florence: loving and uninspired. Her father was a dreamer: a factory manager who felt he should have been a director of the company. He read the Russian classics because he thought it made him appear scholarly. It had taken him two years to finish reading *Anna Karenina* and then he had studied the life of its author, Count Leo Tolstoy. He came across Alexandra Tolstaya,

Tolstoy's daughter, and 'Alexandra' Whitson nearly came to be.

At this point, Sarah's parents had one of the few major rows of their marriage. No daughter of Florence was being given a Russian name: they had stored atomic bombs on Cuba. That marvellous President Kennedy had saved the Western world. Mrs Whitson had dug in and Sarah Florence Whitson entered this world.

She matured quickly. When she was thirteen years old, her mother agreed that Sarah could spend an hour on her own in the shopping centre: they would meet later at the bus station. Savouring her independence, she decided to buy herself an orange drink and a cake in the coffee shop. A rather pleasant man, wearing a clerical collar, came and sat by her. He asked her if she read the Bible, to which she replied, 'Often.' When he enquired as to which was her favourite gospel, she replied, 'The Evangelist, St John.' The man suggested to her that perhaps St Matthew was more interesting. He said he was going to the Gents and he would bring her back another drink. She shook her head and watched as he moved away. She stood up, picked up her bag, left the building and ran and ran and ran.

She reached her mother ten minutes later and decided not to tell her what had happened. Later that night, when she was alone in her bed, Sarah racked her brains as to why she had fled from such a nice man. It took her some time to fathom it out. Then she realised the reason for her reaction to the 'vicar': he had been wearing dirty running shoes. When she looked back on the incident as an adult, she thought this was perhaps the first example of her instinct for spotting a villain: an instinct which was to stand her in good stead on more than one occasion later on in her life.

When she was a teenager, Sarah had a number of friends. She was popular and much sought after. As often as not, though, Sarah preferred to be by herself and to lose herself in the world of books. She particularly relished crime thrillers. She passed her school examinations and then walked the peaks of the Lake District, basing herself at the Outward Bound School in Eskdale. She was trying to work out what she wanted to do with her life. She started work at the Council offices, moved on to becoming a sales assistant in a local shoe shop (amazing how many people didn't wash their feet properly) and then became a doctor's receptionist, with the aim of becoming a medical secretary. During the long hours on reception, Sarah allowed her dreams to surface. One day, she would be Miss Marple, the private investigator created by crime writer, Agatha Christie; the next Inspector Wexford as described by Ruth Rendell; and then she would transform into Dr Kay Scarpetta as brought to life by Patricia Cornwell. She did have a spell as PD James's Adam Dalgliesh, but that soon passed.

Sarah was not sure when she made the decision to apply to the police for a job. Her first marriage had withered away as soon as she and Billy ('William' to his mother) had got out of bed. There was nothing else there.

She enjoyed working in the surgery, though, and knew that, at times, she helped people. But, one night, after a row with one of the doctors at the surgery, who questioned her right to suggest that the child he had just discharged might have meningitis, she went home and drank a bottle of wine. The patient had a mild form of eczema and soon recovered. Sarah did not. She was undone by the suggestion that she was a receptionist and must learn to know her place.

Three nights later she repeated her alcoholic 'self-medication' and emailed her best friend Andrea, whose family had emigrated to Adelaide two years earlier, to tell her she was 'a bit down'.

'Honey,' she responded, 'your place is in the sun, over here. And the fellas...'

Sarah laughed and emailed back: 'Men? That's all I want!'

'Honey, believe me, you need old fellas.'

'What on earth do you mean? Why would I want old guys?'

The email remained unanswered. She was not to know that the phrase Andrea had used implied a suggestion that what her friend needed was a pleasant playtime with some Australian male genitalia.

The next day, Sarah took the plunge and resigned from her job at the surgery, leaving a certain doctor overbooked with appointments, including two known hypochondriacs and 'Mr Angry'; a patient who had turned complaining into an art form.

She applied to join the Hertfordshire constabulary — she didn't know exactly why: perhaps it was simple instinct — and was accepted as a probationary police constable. She fitted in immediately. She loved the uniform: the unflattering black trousers actually enhanced her figure.

She was told to report to Stevenage police station and immediately faced an unpleasant initiation. A constable approached her with a name and address written on a piece of paper and told her to visit the man immediately. She was to collect a sample of his faeces that was needed for a DNA test. The errand had been embarrassing, confusing, and deeply unsavoury. That evening, the same police officer found something unpleasantly pungent smeared over the seat of his motorcycle. The first groping hand to reach for her breasts retired with bruised fingers, and when Sergeant Greengrass called her 'darling', she stood firm.

'I'm not your 'darling', and if you address me like that again, I'll speak to the Inspector.'

The battle lines were drawn. The predators upped the status of the challenge and a book was started on the first officer to bed her. The Sergeant came in at 100/1 against.

***

In her second week, Sarah found herself in a vehicle, screeching to a halt outside some school gates. Her companion, PC Parlin, radioed in to Control announcing their arrival. Then he and Sarah piled out of the patrol car. Sarah's problem was that she shouldn't have been anywhere near there.

She had been instructed by Inspector Mantel to spend a wet, cold Thursday afternoon in December walking around Stevenage, to give the shopkeepers some reassurance that law enforcement was present during their busy Christmas trading period. She was on day three of her five-day period and was feeling sore and miserable.

As Sarah had left his office, Inspector Mantel had called her back.

'Now don't let me down. You better start movin' up town.'

She looked at him in complete amazement. Had he sung it? He waved a hand, indicating that she should be on her way. She left his office, totally baffled.

Sarah walked along the bitterly cold street, feeling unwell, unloved and unhappy. Why would the Inspector tell her to walk to the very furthest point of her patrol area? Was it some kind of test?

Just then, PC Irving Parlin drew up beside her. He was not exactly Brad Pitt, but what the hell!

He stopped the car and invited her to get in. She knew that he was a womaniser and she was a target. She did not object to the flattery and she had just finished another disappointing relationship. At that moment, he stood no chance, but she couldn't help hoping he'd keep trying.

'Hey, sexy, get in!' He had a way with words.

She was cold: she was, in fact, very cold, very wet and very, very achy.

Inspector Mantel had told her that she was to return to the station by three o'clock so that he could discuss her progress. She was halfway through her probationary period and she wanted, more than anything in this world, to be confirmed as a Police Constable. It was two forty-two. She could just about afford to spend five minutes in the warmth of the car and then rush back to the station.

Irving wasted no time. As he moved through the gears and drove away from the town centre, the chat-up began.

'You've got a lovely arse, Sarah,' he started, but was cut off by the radio, paging all vehicles in the area of St Dunstan's School.

PC Parlin quickly called in his location. A 999 call had come in from a local school. There was a report of a fight in the playground and a knife had been seen. PC Parlin snapped on the blues and twos and put his foot down.

'Irving, please. Let me get out!' shouted Sarah.

He ignored her.

They reached the school in under four minutes. For a few seconds, after getting out of the patrol car, they both stood looking around them, taking in what was happening, and working out what needed to be done most urgently.

A lollipop lady had left her crossing and was standing by the school gates, and waved them into the playground. All around the arid asphalt space ran a high wire fence, and all around the fence, their backs pressed as tightly to it as they could manage, stood children and teachers, eyes fixed in terror on the scene in front of them.

Two boys, maybe twelve years old, were facing off against each other, yelling and screaming hysterically. One, smaller but wiry, and with an expression of pure venom on his face, was holding his right arm stiffly in front of him, while the other danced backwards, trying desperately to stay out of his reach. The smaller boy held a knife. There was blood on the blade, and lying at the boys' feet was a white-faced man, blood pouring from a cut across his forehead.

Sarah and PC Parlin raced across the playground, each of them grabbing one of the boys, pulling them apart and trying to restrain them and calm them down. Irving had the boy with the knife, disarmed him and cuffed him with ruthless efficiency. Sarah tackled the bigger boy, who turned on her in a blind rage, biting down on her arm and kicking her feet from under her.

Two additional officers were now on the scene and succeeded in dragging him off her. She heard the sound of ambulances arriving at the school.

Sarah found herself lying by the side of the injured man. He was holding his hands over his face, as blood welled up between his fingers. Sarah saw that he was beginning to shake with shock.

'Are you okay?' she asked. She wanted to keep him talking and conscious until the paramedics got to him. 'I'm Florence. What's your name? What happened?'

She realised that she was gabbling and had given him her middle name.

'I'm Nick. I teach French here.'

They talked together as the paramedics patched him up and prepared to take him to hospital. They wanted to take her too, but she refused, saying she was fine, apart from where she'd got dirt on her trousers when she'd been knocked to the ground.

An hour later, she was given a verbal dressing down by Inspector Mantel. She'd arrived late for her interview, had left her beat and got into a patrol car, and she'd got blood on her uniform.

As she stood up, he said: 'Lord, forgive me for what I do, but if you want out well, it's up to you.'

'Fuck you!' she said to herself as she left his office. 'If I'm sacked then use plain bloody English.' There was still another year to go before she completed her probationary period: things were not looking good. She reached the front enquiry office and was called over by the station manager.

'Sarah, have you heard of a 'Florence'? Bloke here's looking for a police officer called Florence.

New one on me.'

She reached the exit and went through the door. The rain had stopped. He was staring around the street. He had a bandage around his head. He saw her and held out a small bunch of flowers.

'My name's Sarah,' she said.

He looked at her, baffled.

'I'm sorry. I thought I heard you say...'

'Florence. You did. Sarah Florence. For some reason I told you my middle name.'

'Lovely name. From the Latin *florere* which means to flower,' he gasped.

'You said that you teach French?'

'Languages.' He laughed. 'My own Florence Nightingale in my hour of need.'

But he was stumbling forwards, weak and dizzy. They had wanted him to stay in hospital overnight, but he was a man on a mission.

Sarah held him up as he began to fall.

'Time to take you home,' she said.

Early in the New Year, Sarah found herself in the office of Inspector Mantel.

'I have decided, PC Whitson, that it's time for you to understand what policing is all about.'

She realised that there was another person in the office. He came out of the shadows.

'I want you to meet Detective Constable Rodney Windsor.'

The first feature that she noticed was his starched white shirt. Her eyes went up and down from the shining black shoes to the immaculate haircut: number three up the sides and two on top. She held out her hand and he ignored it.

'You will spend four weeks accompanying DC

Windsor. That's all.'

She followed the police officer out of the door, not believing what she was hearing: 'He got mad and he saw red. Andy said, 'Boy, don't lose your head'.'

Within minutes of leaving the Inspector's office, she realised that DC Windsor was expecting her to follow him around like a lapdog. He had only one thought on his mind. He was determined to impress Inspector Mantel and arrest a teenage hoodlum who had, yet again, broken his bail conditions.

Sarah had another man to occupy her thoughts. She had started seeing Nick Rudd, the teacher she had helped in the school playground. He was having a tricky time. The stitches in his forehead had become infected and the parents of the pupil he'd rescued had submitted a formal complaint against the school.

Nick was different. He treated her with respect and was fascinated by her work as a police officer. He taught French and PE and she began to appreciate his dedication.

Sarah loved being herself with him: she could wear casual clothes and did not need to make an effort. The explosion came after three weeks. She had been delayed by a shoplifter who'd made off and had to be apprehended; she was late coming off duty. She went straight to the cinema. Nick blinked when he saw her in uniform. They were soon absorbed in Episode I of *Star Wars*. She fantasised over Ewan McGregor and he imagined Natalie Portman wearing nothing but stockings and a vest.

They arrived back at Nick's flat where they felt 'the Force'. He threw her on the bed and whipped his tie off. Sarah found her wrist secured to the bed head, and discovered that Nick was a rather fit athlete with incredible stamina.

He was the seventh man she had slept with and, she decided, he would be the last. When he admitted that, for him, the police uniform was an aphrodisiac, she knew she had him. She slipped into an Ann Summers sex shop and bought a pair of fur-lined handcuffs.

***

The next day she took a different approach to her companion for the day.

'Go fuck yourself!' were her opening words to DC Windsor. She told him she thought he was pretentious and so far up himself, he probably hadn't seen daylight for a year.

'The thought of spending the day with you is doing my head in,' she added, 'so keep your eyes on the road and bloody shut up.'

DC Rodney Windsor was out of his depth. He tried uttering pleasantries and meaningless comments about the political situation, admitting that he was under pressure because he had failed to locate the missing teenage thug.

'Stop at the cafe in the High Street,' Sarah told him. She slipped quickly out of the car, returning twenty minutes later.

'That'll cost you four coffees and five burgers,' she told him.

'Five!' DC Windsor exclaimed.

'I was hungry,' she said. 'We'll find him at the Cross Lines estate: 8, Melville Road.'

They reached the location. DC Windsor knocked on the door and was met by a torrent of abuse from the mother.

'Thanks, Mrs Ridley. Good of you to ask us in. Just need a quick word with Titus,' said DC Windsor, shouldering past her and leading their way into the house.

A man was sitting in the lounge, smoking something pungent.

'Search the fucking house, you pigs! Titus ain't here.'

They left after a few minutes.

'Shit!' exclaimed Rodney. 'Another bollocking from Inspector Mantel when we get back!'

'He's in there,' said Sarah, deeply regretting not having followed her instincts when they were in the house.

'No, he's not. I'd better report back to Inspector Mantel and get it over with,' said DC Windsor.

'It will do your career good to take Titus with you,' said Sarah. 'Wait outside and the moment you hear me yell, come and get me.'

She walked back to the front door and rang the bell. Almost immediately, the mother opened it. Sarah put her arms around her. They whispered together and then went inside.

Seven minutes later, he heard shouting and went through the door, which PC Whitson had deliberately left ajar. Sarah was on the landing, fighting with a deranged-looking youth. He rushed up the stairs and the two police officers managed to subdue him and get him into the back of the patrol car where his rage subsided.

As they were driving back, DC Windsor asked Sarah how she had known that Titus was hiding in the house.

'What was showing on the TV?' she asked.

'Not really sure. I was attending to my duties.'

'*Byker Grove*, Rodney. Mums don't watch drug gangs.'

Sarah smiled to herself. Duncan was her favourite character and she thought that Declan Donnelly was cute.

'So you knew something,' said DC Windsor.

'There were also three plates on the table and five mugs. Titus had been there with his pals.'

'Oh yes, very good, really terrific.' He gave a silly laugh. 'But what did you say to the mother?' he asked.

'I told her I was suffering from cystitis and needed the loo.'

'Oh, clever you!'

'Rodney,' said Sarah.

'What?'

'Wise up. Relax. You'll be promoted. Just give up the act. And, incidentally, thanks for coming for me. Titus was losing it.'

He slowed as the cars ahead stopped at the traffic lights.

'I'm not really totally obsessive,' he added. 'And I have seen daylight… once or twice.'

'You're okay, Rodney. You just don't need to try so hard. What have you got lined up for the weekend?'

'Aha! Well, she's rather…'

Sarah and Rodney were chatting peaceably, waiting for the lights to change, oblivious to the fact that, showing his inexperience, DC Windsor had failed to handcuff his prisoner.

Titus, though, wasn't one to overlook a golden opportunity. He'd been quietly wriggling closer and closer to the door, and had managed to undo the window lock. Grabbing his chance while the car was stationary and in one swift movement, he wound the window down, reached through, unlocked the back door, hurtled out of the patrol car and made off down the street.

The explosion from Inspector Mantel was toxic. PC Whitson and DC Windsor were banished into the town centre, under strict orders to recapture their missing prisoner, and not to show their faces back in the nick until they'd done so.

As she closed the office door, Sarah heard: 'When he leaves me, he wears a smile now.'

She and Rodney contacted Oscar One and asked that a message was passed to all officers on patrol, and briefed the CCTV Control Room officer about the missing prisoner. They then began their own search on foot, street by street. As they turned into Queensway, Sarah edged closer to her fellow officer.

'Did you hear what he said?'

'Who?'

'Inspector Mantel. He said something about leaving me.'

DC Windsor laughed.

'Nobody's told you, have they, Sarah?'

'Told me what?'

'Reba McEntire.'

'Is that his girlfriend?'

'He wishes she was,' laughed Rodney.

They stopped to help a disabled pensioner who was struggling to get onto a bus.

'So who's Reba McEntire?' asked Sarah.

'She's an American Country and Western singer. A sort of slightly taller Dolly Parton with smaller breasts.'

'Rodney!' exclaimed Sarah. 'I never thought that I'd hear you say such a thing.'

'She's written and performed hundreds of songs. Inspector Mantel is obsessed with her. He went to the States to see her in concert. You heard him say, 'When he leaves me, he wears a smile now'.'

'Yes. That's what he said.'

'Inspector Mantel is no fool. It's followed by 'As soon as he's away from me, in your arms is where he wants to be'. It's from a song called *Does he love you*?' Rodney chuckled. 'I bet you've heard him saying 'Now don't let me down, you better start movin' uptown.' It's from her best song ever, which is called "*Fancy*".'

But, at that moment, a young offender called Titus came round the corner and immediately spotted the police officers. The chase lasted 200 yards, until DC Windsor brought him down with a flying tackle.

Sarah arrived breathless and fell across them both.

'Well done, Rodney,' she gasped.

'Played on the wing for Harrow,' he said.

He looked down at his captive.

'You're nicked!' he said.

That evening, over dinner, Sarah was telling her favourite French teacher all about her day.

As she finished, he stood up and moved over to her, bending down to hold her by the arms. He leant into her. She could smell his aftershave and feel the warmth of his breath on her cheek.

'You're nicked!' he echoed softly.

'I am,' Sarah smiled up at him. 'I am indeed.'

A NIGHT OF PAIN

31 December, 1999

The call she was dreading came in the middle of November. That morning in bed, she had gazed down at the sleeping Nick, and traced her finger gently over the fading scar on his forehead. It was that wound which had brought them together, she thought, with a mixture of regret and wonder: regret that he'd been hurt; wonder at the happiness he'd brought her. She was due to see Inspector Mantel at eleven-thirty, but was finding it hard to drag herself away from Nick. She was now intoxicated with affection for her husband, and loved their intense, exciting relationship.

In recent weeks, as the date of her interview drew closer, she had experienced mood swings: one day she'd be tense and touchy; the next, confident and indifferent. If they refused her, so what? It would be their loss: she'd start a new career. Perhaps she'd go into teaching.

She sauntered up the stairs and knocked on the door; she responded to the command to enter.

'Yes. PC Whitson, come in.'

'PC Rudd, sir, I was married five months ago.'

'Yes. This is Inspector Avery Western.' He paused. 'I have some bad news for you.'

Her stomach sank and she slumped into the chair. She felt sure that she had failed her probationary period. She was not to be confirmed as a police officer. Nick had prepared for the worst and promised her a Christmas break in the sun.

'Yes, bad news. You'll be disappointed, I'm afraid.'

'I'll cope, sir.'

'I'm sorry to have to tell you that I'm leaving Stevenage.' He stood up and she wondered if he was going to salute the picture of the Queen on the opposite wall. 'I've been accepted as a Chief Inspector in the Met. I go tomorrow. I can't tell you any more: bit hush-hush, you understand.' He held out his arm. 'This is your new boss.'

She looked at the tall, fair-haired man. He seemed to have a nervous twitch in his left eye.

Sarah remained seated on the chair and waited.

'Congratulations, sir,' she said.

'Yes. Rather unexpected. I'm sure you'll get on with Inspector Western.' He paused. 'That's all.'

Sarah remained seated and felt confused.

'There's nothing else you want to say to me, sir?'

'Oh, your confirmation. Well done, PC Rudd. You're through with flying colours. You have a great future ahead of you.'

Inspector Western approached her and shook her hand.

'Congratulations, PC Rudd. I look forward to working with you.'

She stood up and absorbed the silence. She held out her hand and took it back again, then looked at Inspector Mantel, smiled, and moved towards the door. She hesitated and turned round: 'One honest heart that I can believe in,' she sang in a whisper.

'Don't tell me, PC Rudd,' exclaimed her departing boss. 'She recorded it last year. Reba at her best. Give me time...'

'It shouldn't be so hard, finding one honest heart,' sang Sarah softly.

'Got it! It's called '*One Honest Heart*'.'

'Well done, sir.' She laughed. 'And good luck.'

As the door closed, Inspector Mantel turned to his companion.

'She's special, that one, Avery. Bit wild but as committed as I've seen.'

'With one honest heart, Renning,' he chuckled.

'With a big heart, Avery. She's going to be a copper through and through.'

***

PC Sarah Rudd knew the bastard was going to hurt the girl. He was pissed as a newt and as high as a kite. Sarah's mind flashed back to the Monday morning briefing: new levels of a cheap, and deadly, crack cocaine were flooding Stevenage. It looked like this lad had sucked up a fair whack of it. He was certainly twitchy enough. It was 31 December and the girl would probably start the New Year on a stretcher in the A & E unit at the Lister.

She could hear her Inspector telling her to take care. This was after he had instructed Sarah to make the arrest. Okay, she'd completed her two-year probationary period. Yes, she was now a proper, fully fledged police constable. But shouldn't it be Inspector Avery Western going into the alley, in all his high-potential, development-scheme glory, rather than her vastly less experienced self? She accepted he was fed-up and longing to get back to the warmth of his home: his family had now completed their move from

Yorkshire. But that didn't quite disguise the possibility that her new Inspector was, as she'd suspected, just a bit of a coward.

'Arrest that man!' he had ordered. Less than straightforward, since the offender had his arm around the girl's throat.

When she'd taken the plunge, left her cosy, sheltered, boring life at the doctor's, and joined the force, she had fitted in as a probationary police constable immediately. She loved the uniform, even the bulky black trousers. She'd been a bit annoyed the day before when she'd been forced to add another notch so that the belt would fasten comfortably. Too many pastries from the party when she'd passed her probation. Worth it, though.

She loved being a member of the Hertfordshire Constabulary and now she was through her probationary period, she liked her posting to the challenging town of Stevenage, which was by no means a sleepy backwater, as the scene before her proved.

Sarah was now focused on the situation and decided that she needed to know the young man's name. She was keeping eye contact with the unknown victim in his grasp, who was clearly scared witless. Sarah froze. She'd just realised the man was holding a knife to the girl's throat. She whispered to her Inspector. He'd noticed the weapon too and was trying to work out how to radio for reinforcements without escalating the situation.

'Matt, put the knife down,' she called out.

'Who's fucking Matt, copper?'

'Well, you're good looking. All handsome men are called Matt.'

'This one ain't, bitch. Donovan, that's me. Fucking silly name. Some pop singer my mum liked.'

'My name's Sarah.' She paused. "*The Hurdy Gurdy Man*,' she said.

'You takin' the piss, copper?'

'Donovan sang it, around the seventies. Great lyrics.' She moved her feet slightly. 'Let her go, Don.'

'Donovan! Don't you never fuckin' shorten it, bitch.'

'Let her go,' repeated Sarah, in the same clear, even tone.

The inspector put his hand on her shoulder, but she shrugged it off. They both listened to the aggressor.

'She went with Marty last night; shagged him in the pavilion.' He spat on the street. 'My best buddy.'

Inspector Western and Constable Rudd had been nearing a notoriously troublesome public house when they had become aware of a youth dragging a girl by her hair: she was screaming out with the pain. Sarah went forward and the young man had retreated up a side passageway, locked his arms around the girl and had now produced a knife, which he held to her throat. Sarah Rudd and her inspector were frozen to the spot, not daring to move. They were all getting drenched in the bitter evening rain and the girl's lips were turning blue. The spray from the passing traffic obscured the small group from view.

'Donovan,' said Constable Rudd, 'let her go, please.' She paused and wiped the rain from her face. 'What's your name?' she asked the girl, addressing her directly.

'Helena,' she whispered.

'Hang on, Helena. We'll soon have you out of

here.'

At twenty-nine years old, Sarah was already worldly wise. From the moment she had first put on the uniform, she had assumed an air of authority. She was going to need all her presence and all her authority in the next half-hour because Donovan would, she felt sure, put someone's life in danger at some point.

The two police officers now found themselves in a stalemate. The serrated edge of the combat knife, within an inch of Helena's throat, paralysed them. They were whispering to each other but Inspector Western had never been in a hostage situation before. There seemed to be a gulf between theory learned in the classroom, and practice in this filthy, wet, cold street. The rain had turned to hail and fell with increasing ferocity. Despite the festive season, the foul weather was keeping most people indoors. They heard laughter from across the road as someone opened the door and hurried into the warmth of the pub.

'Why don't you two fuck off?' yelled Donovan.

'Not without Helena,' said Sarah Rudd.

The girl whimpered, but found that just made the boy tighten his grip on her.

Sarah sensed that the Inspector was going to speak.

'No, sir,' she whispered. 'He's relating to me. It's our only hope.'

She had calculated that there were three possible outcomes: the first was that she managed to persuade Donovan to hand over his weapon; the second that she succeeded in taking the knife off him; and the third that something unexpected happened.

'Are you aware, Donovan, that Stevenage was the first town ever to have black bags for refuse collection?' she asked.

'What was that, bitch?' shouted the youth.

'I read it in a guidebook. Amazing, don't you think? Stevenage leading the country in clearing up rubbish!'

She realised that the Inspector was trying to speak into his radio, unnoticed.

'Sir,' Sarah urged insistently, 'please stay still.'

'May I remind you that I'm the senior officer...'

'You sent me in, sir. It's my situation.'

Constable Sarah Rudd was setting the scene for the rest of her career: a willingness to challenge authority if the situation required. That was fine, provided she achieved the right result.

'Were you born here, Donovan?' she asked.

'Stop asking me fucking daft questions.'

'Right. I'll ask Helena. How are you feeling, Helena?'

'Scared,' she replied.

'Don't worry, I'm going to get you out of here,' Sarah answered confidently. Inside, she felt sick with fear. She remembered that she had, in fact, been sick that morning. She had decided it was due to Nick's seafood risotto and the peppers and onions that he loved to add.

'We'll get out of this together, Helena,' Sarah repeated. 'Is he hurting you?'

'Shut your gob, pig!' ordered Donovan.

'As you say, Donovan,' said Sarah. 'Do you mind if I put my coat over Helena. She's shivering with cold.'

'Chuck it over here, you cow.'

Sarah sent it over and Donovan wrapped it around

his girlfriend.

Sarah felt Inspector Western pulling at her arm.

'We need to do something,' he hissed.

'What would you like me to do, sir?'

'Er, disarm him.'

The storm, which had drenched the town earlier in the day, was now abating and there was more light from the west. The local church bells announced that it was eleven-thirty.

Sarah noticed that when Donovan spoke he pulled the knife imperceptibly away from Helena's throat. She reviewed her options: he was not going to hand over his weapon, there was unlikely to be a sudden event, and so she was left with her need to take the knife off him. The Inspector's radio buzzed and the caller decided he was engaged on routine matters.

'Donny, please stop holding me so tight.'

Sarah looked on in surprise as she noticed that he immediately eased his grip on Helena.

'What'd you see in fuckin' Marty? Tell me, Helly.'

'I made a mistake, Donny. I love you, babe.'

New dark clouds appeared and the rain came pouring down. The traffic seemed to stop and there was a strange stillness.

Inspector Western was getting restless and Sarah was concerned that he would do something precipitous and quite soon. She hissed at him. 'Sir, hold on, please.'

'Do you really love him, Helena?' she asked.

'What's it fucking well to do with you, bitch?' shouted Donovan.

'Yeah, copper,' said Helena. 'You leave me and Donny alone.'

Suddenly, the pair parted and Donovan took a

stride towards Sarah, holding the knife in front of him. He tensed his arm ready to strike when Inspector Western leaped forward. The blade sliced across his hand severing muscle and sinew. The police officer was thrown off-balance just as the assailant's knife penetrated Constable Rudd's clothing, aiming for her gut.

***

A police officer was waiting outside the door to the hospital room. Sarah was attached to a heart monitor and an oxygen mask. A doctor was reading the digital results. Nick was sitting holding her hand. Chief Superintendent Marian Musgrove opened the door gently and stood at the end of Sarah's bed.

'I need to speak to Mr Rudd,' said Dr Sally Patel.

The Chief Superintendent began to move away until she was stopped by a request from Nick that she stay.

'As you wish,' said the doctor. 'Mr Rudd, when the man lunged with the knife, your wife experienced what we think was an adrenaline rush. In basic terms, the body's defences swarmed to protect her and it was too much for her system. She collapsed and, in the mayhem of the moment, it was thought that she had been stabbed. The knife ripped her clothing, and she received some nasty bruising to her abdomen. We've conducted a full examination and there are no internal injuries.' The doctor smiled. 'Nothing to worry about at all, I promise. If she'd not been wearing her body armour it would have been a very different story.'

Sarah stirred and opened her eyes. Dr Patel lifted

the mask away from her face. Nick wiped her forehead. She moaned and then smiled.

'Helena, how is she?' she asked.

'Fine, Constable Rudd,' said Chief Superintendent Musgrove. 'She's down at the station giving a statement.'

'And Inspector Western, ma'am?'

'He's in theatre. They're going to have to do extensive micro-surgery on his hand. He's chirpy, though. Before they put him under he was talking about citing you for a commendation.'

'Just being a copper, Ma'am.'

'Mrs Rudd needs a lot of rest,' said the doctor, 'but we'll probably let her go home tomorrow.'

The senior policeman held up her hand.

'I'm off. You take good care of yourself, Constable Rudd. That young lad, Donovan Royle, he's been nicked. He's got form. With any luck, he won't be out and about for quite a while now.' The Chief Superintendent hesitated. 'We'll talk again, but we're proud of you. Your courage in a one-for-one is...'

'I think not,' said the doctor.

'You were there?'

'No, of course not, but I can tell you that Mrs Rudd was not alone.'

She looked across at Nick Rudd who nodded. He did not object to Chief Superintendent Musgrove hearing what was about to be revealed.

'Mrs Rudd was not alone,' repeated Dr Sally Patel with a smile on her face. 'You're four months pregnant, Mrs Rudd, and everything's fine. Once we realised you were pregnant, we carried out scans to ensure that no harm had come to the baby. It's absolutely fine. We have the pictures for you to see if you'd like.'

Nick looked at the doctor. 'It's fine?'

'You want to know?'

He nodded.

The doctor showed him the photographs of his new baby and whispered something to him.

Nick turned back to the bed.

'It's a girl?' Sarah guessed, as he bent over and kissed her tenderly.

'Might be a boy,' he laughed.

***

Benzoylmethylecgonine, otherwise known as cocaine, is an extract of the coca plant: a stimulant and addictive. It can be inhaled through the nostrils, injected into the bloodstream, or, in the form of crack cocaine, smoked in a pipe.

Donovan Royle reeled out of the Gents, white powder around his nostrils and scattered down his shirt. He was a hero and relishing his newfound status. Helena went to him, and, holding his arm, steered him back to the table where they were all sitting.

'Thought you'd been locked up,' said a man at the next table. The pub was full and they were all crowded together. Two youths passed the table and the one accidently spilled some of his lager over Donovan's jacket. He looked aghast and immediately apologised.

'Donnie mate, so sorry.'

'Pigs fell off their fucking chairs,' continued Donovan. 'The magistrate said I wasn't a fucking danger.'

Helena kissed him and then announced that her Donny was going to concentrate on getting a job.

'Just one bit of unfinished fucking business,' he said.

'Donny, please, you promised,' she pleaded.

He pushed her aside.

'No fucking pig gets the better of me.'

THE ACID TEST

14 February, 2000

Donovan Royle rarely read the printed word beyond the football pages. He did, however, prick up his ears when Helena read out the headlines from *The Sun* newspaper. He had already ogled the scantily clad Page Three girl, who claimed to be enthralled by the news of the release of Jonathan Aitken from prison. The former Conservative MP had been set free after serving seven of his eighteen months sentence following his conviction for perjury. She had a proposal for him: 'Laylah from Epping would love to spend time behind bars with Jonathan'.

'Donny,' cried Helena. 'Listen to this: "Bollywood Babe-to-be seeks Revenge"''.

'Wot?'

'It's horrible, Donny.' She was staring at the photograph and held it up for him to see. One side of the girl's face had been destroyed.

'Fuck me!' exclaimed Donovan. 'What's it say?'

Helena read out the story: 'Chucked! Bollywood Babe-to-be seeks Revenge.

'Twenty-three-year-old budding fashionista Haseena Hussain, of Mumbai, India, has enlisted the support of human rights organisation Acid Survivors Trust International in her fight against sleaze-bag, former employer Pravnar Patel. In February, 1999, Patel, a sixty-three-year-old widower, told Haseena he was promoting her from her desk job to his bed as the next Mrs Patel. Haseena had other plans and politely told pervy Patel she was off to Bollywood as a fashion designer. Patel followed Haseena to her home that night and hurled acid in her face. Said brave Haseena: 'It was horrible. It hurt so much. I couldn't see. I couldn't do anything. I know there were people around, but no one wanted to get involved.' Without witnesses, police say they are unable to press charges. Now ASTI is hoping to make them change their minds and prosecute poisonous Patel.'

'Do you think she might like me to sort the bastard out, Helly?'

'He's in India, Donny.'

'Where's that?'

***

He kicked her again and she laughed. It was Monday, it was cold and it was the day when lovers shared their secrets. Sarah's son was particularly lively despite the snow and ground frost in the world outside. Police Constable Sarah Rudd was coming to the end of her early shift. She was anticipating taking off her tight-fitting uniform and dressing in comfortable maternity clothes. She would be home just after four o'clock. By agreement with her husband, they would open their Valentine's Day cards and share an early evening supper together.

She left the police station a bit downcast. She had, during her coffee break, read in the newspaper that Diana Ross had divorced her billionaire, Norwegian husband of fourteen years, Arne Naess. She bought her latest album, *Every Day is a New Day*, for

Nick and she had written inside the card: Track two says it all.

As she strolled along the back street to her car, she hummed the words of '*Love is all that matters*' to herself:

'*We all have one heart*
And one heart needs another
Love is all that matters
Love is all that matters
It matters after all.'

She was two seconds too late to sense the body odour behind her. As she realised the danger that lurked, and tried to spin round, she felt a pain as she was hit in the base of her back with a blunt implement.

'Fuckin' look ahead, bitch! Turn round and I'll kill ya!'

'Donovan, don't be silly,' she said as she recognised his distinctive voice.

'See that door ahead? Push it open!' he ordered.

Sarah followed his instructions. She was trying to work out what was being prodded into her back. She did as she was told and found herself in a derelict room, with a table and two chairs. There was a container on the table. He kicked the door closed behind him and told her to sit down. He sat opposite and grabbed the cup.

'Not so fuckin' clever now, are you, copper?'

He had now produced a broom handle and was waving it in the air with his left hand.

'Enough of this, Donovan,' snapped Sarah. 'You know I'm going to have to arrest you again.'

'You'll do nothing, cunt.' He lifted the cup up. 'Know what this is? Acid. Got it? And it's going all over your fuckin' face.'

Sarah froze to the spot. She was not to know, but it was nitric acid and would almost certainly blind her. A small amount had spilt onto the surface of the table and she could see corrosion starting to eat into the wood.

Whatever Sarah thought might now develop could never have prepared her for what happened next.

'Take your clothes off.' His voice was cold and calm.

'Donovan, I'm six months pregnant, and it's bloody cold today,' she pleaded.

'You're fuckin' gorgeous, bitch. My Helly's too thin. You've got lots of shape. I want to see your tits.'

'You can't. It's freezing and I've my baby to think about.'

He lifted the cup and started getting off the chair.

Sarah stood up and took off her coat. She sat down again, her legs like jelly. Her mind was racing. There was no way she could rush him: the acid could do untold damage even if she deflected his throw. She could not reach her radio. She would not be missed for several hours: Nick was only too aware of the demands made on his wife. An agreed arrival time at home was merely an estimate. She had their son inside her.

'I'll undo the buttons of my blouse. That's all I'll do, Donovan.'

She started at the top and released four of them, one by one, as slowly as she dared.

Donovan was hypnotised by the flesh being revealed. She was wearing a flesh-coloured bra. She watched his eyes and undid another button. His right hand remained firmly around the cup of acid. She reached the top of her abdomen revealing her pregnant bump.

'Take it off,' he ordered. His eyes were dazzled by the pink allure.

'No,' said Sarah.

'I don't have to throw it all at once, bitch. Perhaps a few spots on your lump. Should give your kid a surprise.'

Sarah stood up, removed her blouse and took off her bra. She never took her eyes off Donovan's face.

'Fuck me. You should be on Page Three,' he laughed.

'Donovan,' said Sarah. 'I need to pee.'

'Fuckin' wait.'

Sarah was elated. He was talking about the future. It was her first victory.

'I can't. I'm pregnant. You can't control these things. I'm about to make quite a mess.'

Suddenly, she grasped her hands around her stomach.

'Braxton Hicks,' she groaned.

'What you fucking talkin' 'bout?' yelled Donovan as Sarah doubled up in pain.

'My muscles are squeezing, Donovan. The doctor told me. It's called Braxton Hicks contractions: they're brought on by a full bladder. Donovan, please, I must pee.'

Donovan was beginning to panic. He had not anticipated this. He looked around the room. In one corner was a cupboard.

'Go over there,' he pointed as he picked up the acid. 'I'll be the other side. One false move and you'll

41

get the whole lot over you.'

She stood up and put her blouse back on. Victory number two. She had created movement and managed to partially re-clothe herself. She did as she was told, passed water over the floor, made some noises and went back to the chair. He sat down opposite her. Her pains disappeared as quickly as they had come.

They sat looking at each other for a few moments.

'How's your mum?' asked Sarah.

'Take your skirt off,' said Donovan.

'Mrs Royle. She named you after the singer.'

'Wish she hadn't,' he said.

'I like your name, Donovan. You're right as well. If I remember, only Helena is allowed to shorten it.'

'Calls me Donny. Even if I smack her, she says it.'

'Do you enjoy fucking her, Donovan?'

'Mind your own fucking business, copper.'

'That's not fair, Donovan. I'm sitting here, I've shown you my breasts and you won't let me ask about Helena.'

This marked victory three. She noticed that he was easing his grip on the cup.

'She's pathetic. Just opens her legs and tells me she loves me.'

'What do you want her to do?' asked Sarah.

'Mind your own business, copper.'

'Tell me, Donovan. You mentioned Page Three. You were talking about *The Sun* newspaper.'

'UNDO YOUR FUCKING BUTTONS!' yelled Donovan.

She did as she was told. She had rounded red nipples.

'I'm just interested, Donovan. Why do men look at

Page Three girls every day?'

He did not reply. Sarah thought that his left hand was now beneath the table. She suspected this was a partial victory. She had to get him to hurt with desire. Taking her skirt off was an option, but the thought of doing so revolted her.

'Why are you looking at my breasts?' she asked.

'I'm not. Don't you call me a pervert!' he shouted.

Each exchange scored a victory. Sarah was getting him worked up and angry. He had regained his firm grip on the cup of acid.

'There's nothing wrong with looking at a woman's body, Donovan. In fact, I'm quite flattered,' she said.

'My mum thrashed me,' said Donovan.

Here was victory five and it was a big one.

'That was wrong of her, Donovan. She probably did so because she loved you. What had you done?'

'She found a magazine under my bed.'

'What sort of magazine?' Sarah smiled and pulled her blouse around her.

'You know. Bought it at school... porno. That stuff.'

'Do you use that sort of material now, Donovan?'

'Helly gets me DVDs. The girls trade them between themselves.'

Sarah now stood up and got away with it. She sat down again and did up a button.

'Girls are obsessed with penis size, Donovan.'

'How do you know that, copper?'

'Is Helena pleased with yours, Donovan?'

There was total silence and PC Sarah Rudd wondered if she had pushed him too far. He was still holding the cup of acid but his attention was shifting from her chest to her skirt. Whenever she managed to divert his gaze, he loosened his hold, but it was never for more than a second or two.

'I told Helly I'd get you for what you did to me.'

'So this is about proving yourself to Helena, is it, Donovan?'

'I don't need to prove nothin'.'

'So why go to prison? The magistrate told you it was your last chance.' Sarah breathed out slowly. Her plan was in tatters. She had used up all the sex she dare. His mind seemed to be drifting.

'What makes a day a good one for you, Donovan?' she asked.

Donovan Royle looked at PC Rudd.

'Can't get a job. My record stops me. Helly tells me to keep trying.'

'She's right, Donovan.'

'Do you know how long a day is, copper?'

'Tell me, Donovan. What's your usual routine?'

'Get up late, row with my mother, find Helly, shag her, go to the pub, spend the afternoon with my mates, find some grub and have some fun in the evening. We go to the Arsenal when they're at home and to Spurs for a fight.'

'Donovan, may I please put my bra back on?' asked Sarah.

'Do what you fuckin' want. Your tits are crap.'

'How about joining the army?' she asked.

'I was turned down. I've got fuckin' perforated eardrums. My head will blow up if I jump out of a plane. They wanted to send me to a specialist, but I told them to stuff it.'

'So what will you do when you come out of prison?' asked Sarah.

'Fuckin' catch me first, copper.'

'Donovan, if you throw the acid, every policeman in Hertfordshire will be looking for you. You'll be behind bars in hours.'

'No choice, copper. Must prove myself to Helly.'

'You do have a choice.'

'I've no fucking choice. Can't get work; no education; army don't want me.'

'So you flog cocaine to find the money to booze on.' Sarah pointed with her hand. 'Top of your pocket, Donovan. White stains.'

'What else can I do?' he asked.

It was a good question, but at that moment in time PC Rudd did not care. Her son was kicking and she was feeling unwell.

'You've got everything,' said Donovan.

'Have I?' asked Sarah.

'Job, bloke, you're pregnant.'

'Yes. Life's a bundle of fun, Donovan.'

'Why did you interfere with me and Helly, bitch?'

'It's my job, Donovan. It's what I do.'

'She'd shagged Marty. She needed a smack.'

'You held a knife to her throat.'

'Yeah, but I wouldn't have used it, not on Helly. You bloody got in the way. You and that poncy bloke.' Donovan laughed. 'Got what he was asking for.'

'You sliced his hand rather badly, Donovan. He was trying to help your girlfriend.'

'Teach'd 'im a fuckin' lesson.'

Sarah groaned inwardly as her stomach rumbled.

'So when does the violence stop, Donovan?' she asked.

'What you talkin' about?'

'You throw the acid over me. You go to prison for

a long time. Helena goes off with another fellow. Doesn't sound good to me.'

'What do I do, bitch?'

'Only you can make that decision, Donovan.'

He looked at PC Sarah Rudd and wiped his eyes.

'I ain't got no one. Never knew me dad. Not sure me mum knows who he was. Will you help me?'

'No, Donovan. I'm going to arrest you and put you in prison.'

'Let's say this never happened.'

'But it has. It's me today; who might it be tomorrow?'

'How long will I get?' he asked in a voice which betrayed his growing uncertainty.

'That's for the magistrate to decide, but you're beginning to think straight. Do you think Helena will wait for you?'

Donovan gave her question some considerable thought. 'Go and fuck yourself, copper. You should have left us alone.'

He continued to hold on to the cup of nitric acid. He was looking down at the floor.

The ending came quickly as he exhausted his options. Donovan stood up. 'I'll go and hand meself in,' he said. 'No fucking choice now, 'av I?' He stared at her. 'Bitch, your tits are lovely!'

He slammed through the door, leaving Sarah adjusting her clothing and reaching for her radio. She found a piece of wood on the floor. She picked it up and dropped it into the cup. It hissed and disappeared in a cloud of acidic smoke.

***

46

As she opened the front door to her home, Nick was waiting for her. He had managed to slow the oven down on receiving her phone call from the police station and was now ready with the roast gammon and vegetables.

'You don't look so good, darling,' he said as he guided her into their lounge. He handed her a bunch of flowers. He had found his present.

'Number three has been playing up,' she said.

Nick was now aware that there were occasions when he did not ask his wife questions about her work.

'Can I tell you about Ryland?' he asked.

She sipped her wine. She would allow herself just half a glass and then she'd lie to the doctor.

'Who's Ryland?' she murmured.

'He's a good lad: a rugby player. I think he's good enough for the County squad.'

'Fascinating,' she said as Diana Ross was suggesting that 'love is all that matters'.

'The PE master thinks he shirks the important tackles.'

'Does he?' she asked as 'Love is all' rang out.

'He was playing this afternoon in a trial and the other side had this huge gorilla playing in the centre. He broke through and Ryland was left on his own.'

Nick downed his drink and poured Sarah some water.

'He missed it and Nick Rudd has been told to concentrate on being a French teacher?' she laughed.

'He flattened him. Best tackle I've seen this year.'

'Good lad,' murmured Sarah.

'Life's like that, isn't it?'

'Like what, Nick?'

'We make them do tackle practice all the time, but we still weren't certain about Ryland. Then came that one moment: he had nowhere to go, it was his big opportunity, he took it. You might say that it was his key test.'

'Bully for him!' said Sarah.

'It would have been a bitter pill to swallow if he had flunked it.'

Diana Ross was also offering some of her thoughts:

After all that we've been through
It comes down to one simple truth.

Nick stood and looked out of the window. It was starting to snow.

Sarah lowered her head.

'I suppose you could call it an acid test,' she murmured quietly as her son finally settled down inside her.

***

Acid Survivors Trust International

Acid violence is the deliberate use of acid to attack another human being. The victims of acid violence are overwhelmingly women and children, and attackers often target the head and face in order to maim, disfigure and blind. The act rarely kills but causes severe physical, psychological and social scarring, and victims are often left with no legal recourse, limited access to medical or psychological assistance, and without the means to support themselves. Acid violence is a worldwide phenomenon that is not restricted to a particular race, religion or geographical location.

Acid Survivors Trust International (ASTI) is the only organisation whose sole purpose is to work towards the end of acid violence across the world. Recognising the need for local knowledge and expertise in order to combat acid violence effectively, ASTI founded and continues to support the development of six partner organisations in Bangladesh, Cambodia, Pakistan, Nepal, Uganda and India. It also works with UN agencies, NGOs and strategic partners from across the world to increase awareness of acid violence and develop effective responses at the national and international level.

To learn more about how ASTI and its partners have helped acid survivors, please go to www.acidviolence.org

THE MORAL MAZE

October, 2000

Its local name is *Mongo ma Ndemi* which means 'Mountain of Greatness'. Most maps show it as Mount Cameroon: 13,255 feet from sea level to its volcanic top; a long way for the molten lava to flow down to the Gulf of Guinea and into the Atlantic Ocean. It erupted on 14 June 2000, at exactly the same time that PC Sarah Rudd was deciding that she absolutely would not scream.

She was being held down by an invisible force. The average human body has 642 muscles and every one of them hurt. She was aching: what had the bastard injected into her arm? Why was she in a strange place? She had lost all sense of time since they'd carried her off, perhaps six, seven, eight hours ago.

She was dreaming of a room with colours and figures and bells. But then there was an even greater spasm of pain: she did not deserve this. She was a copper patrolling the streets of Stevenage, a fast-growing town north of London. She already had a developed sense of danger and she had not seen this coming. That hectoring Inspector Mantel, now with the Met, had made her read reports about abduction and abuse, but that'd never prepared her for this.

Would he, in the midst of the danger she was facing, have turned to his obsession? Would he have recalled the words of Reba McEntire's '*I'm a Survivor*'? The words echoed in her head: 'I don't believe in self-pity, it only brings you down.'

Even more pain racked her body. Her eyes sprang open. There were lights blinding her. She clenched her eyes tight shut again. 'When the deck is stacked against me, I just play a different game.'

She tried to force herself to relax but this was something unbelievably different. She'd never known pain like it.

She realised she was breathing more easily. Was it over? Had he stopped torturing her? She was beginning to feel better. The pain seemed to be ebbing away. Why had he turned her on her side? And then she was flat on her back and a volcano of agony hit her. She clenched her teeth: her lips had blood on them. She would not cry out. Never, ever. It was getting worse. He was pressing on her. She could take no more: she felt torn apart… and then it was over.

Marcus Charles Rudd had entered the world; all six pounds, five ounces of him.

***

Inspector Avery Western was enjoying having an attractive, well-rounded police constable at his side. PC Rudd had regained her figure following the birth of her son. She made him feel important. She was respectful and attentive: he was certain that she was learning from his views on modern policing methods. He had taken an advantage of a gap in his diary to leave his desk and accompany her on patrol, to 'show her the ropes' as he put it to himself.

They turned away from the town centre and strolled casually towards the bus station. They were wearing coats because of the autumn winds. Gradually, they reached an area of terraced housing populated by immigrants and long-established Irish families.

'Strength and tolerance, PC Rudd,' murmured the Inspector, continuing the lecture he had been doling out quietly to Sarah Rudd ever since they'd left the station. 'We are responsible for civil order and we must understand the reality of the situation where all sorts of people are having to live all jumbled up together. The *quid pro quo*, so to speak, is that they must recognise that we favour no one. All our citizens are equal.'

'Absolutely, sir.'

He was deflected from theorising further as the sound of shouting came out of the 24/7 Asian Convenience Store. Within seconds, a woman carrying a bag ran straight into them, pursued by a rotund shopkeeper waving a wooden baton.

***

Nick was already devoted to his sixteen-week-old son. He even changed the odd nappy, although fatherhood had had a strange effect on his sense of smell, which often meant he was at the far end of the house when Marcus's nappy needed attention. The baby listened with rapt attention as his father explained why the killing of twelve Israeli soldiers in the West Bank was destabilising the peace process, and why Russian troops had left Serbia, and gurgled his agreement that coach Kevin Keegan had to go after England's 0–1 defeat to Germany at Wembley.

Nick was entirely unprepared for his wife's question. His concentration was alternating between his son and her loose-fitting skirt, which seemed to be revealing more than usual of her seductive thighs.

'Are all your pupils equal, Nick?' she asked.

'You mean all 866?' he replied.

'Yes. Are they all the same?'

Nick took Marcus, kissed his cheek, and placed him in the cot. 'We'll discuss Arsenal's selection problems tomorrow,' he whispered.

'Are all pupils equal?' she repeated. Much to his delight, she had now stretched out on the sofa and her skirt had risen even further.

'So what has led to this philosophical question from PC Rudd?' he asked.

She sipped her coffee. 'Today, my Inspector gave me a lecture about all our citizens being equal. Pompous git!'

'And this has provoked your question?' he asked, slightly surprised. His wife was nothing if not unpredictable.

'We were passing an Asian shop when we apprehended this woman. She came running out and managed to crash into us. The shop owner followed and went ballistic. 'White trash!' he was screaming.'

'Was his name Mr Patel?'

Sarah laughed. 'Mr Saleem Nazar, to be specific,' she said. 'But I take the point. He's been robbed almost every week recently and was held up late at night by two yobbos looking for booze. They scared him.'

'So what happened?'

'We went back to the store and the woman

claimed that Mr Nazar had threatened her with a stick and she had run out in fear. The Inspector asked her if he could look into her bag and she agreed. When he did, he discovered twelve tins of canned meat.'

'So you arrested her?'

'She went nuts, Nick. She claimed Mr Nazar had planted the goods in her bag. She said she always buys her children fresh meat.' Sarah stretched out. 'So, yes, we arrested her and took her back to the station. She's now in the system. She'll be fined. I managed to talk to her in the cells. She'll lose some of her benefits. She has three girls from two different fathers, but now has a more permanent partner who has his own daughter. I got the impression they are trying to make a go of it.'

'Sarah, excuse me for saying so, but this sounds like an everyday story of policing.'

She got up to check that Marcus was asleep, then went into the kitchen. She opened a bottle of lager, poured it into a glass and handed it to her husband.

'Inspector Western called me into his office. He asked me how I felt about the case. To be honest, I'd not given it that much thought. I'm a copper, Nick. The world can sort out its own bloody problems.'

'But you liked the woman?'

She took the glass of lager out of his hand and put it on the table. She put her arms around his neck and kissed him.

'She's trying to get her life together. I believed her.'

'So what's this all about, Sarah?'

She returned to the sofa.

'I don't understand why Inspector Weston called me back to his office and then lectured me on his views about policing and the people. I'd heard enough when we were out on patrol. He went on about how important it is that all the people in Stevenage believe that the police treat everybody the same. He said he could have let the woman off but he had to support Mr Nazar.'

'Sarah, I'm lost: either she shoplifted or she didn't; end of story.'

She tugged her skirt down her legs. 'So, there are 866 pupils at your school?'

'Yes,' replied Nick.

'Are they all equal?'

'Yes, no question. We treat them all the same.'

'But you make them take examinations?'

'I don't. The system does. What's your point?'

'That's not equal. Some will have a better chance than others.'

'You mean the ones I teach,' he laughed. 'But seriously, Sarah, there's a difference between everyone being treated the same and everyone being the same. Of course everyone's different: the crucial thing is to show that 'different' doesn't mean more or less important.'

She leaped up and went over to him. She loved her fair-minded, thoughtful, sensible husband. Telling him to stay exactly where he was, she re-appeared a few minutes later wearing her police officer's uniform and waving the pair of fur-lined handcuffs. The top three buttons of her blouse were undone.

As they lay together an hour later, Sarah suddenly shot up in the bed.

'Nick!' she exclaimed.

'Again?' he murmured, hopefully.

'There were no cans of meat in the bag.'

He sat up and realised that Marcus was crying in

the corner of their room. He got out of bed and soon settled him down again. Sarah was sitting upright, staring straight ahead of her.

'She ran into us. We went back to Mr Nazar's shop. I carried the bag because Inspector Western had taken it off her. There was nothing in it. Just some empty carriers and an umbrella.'

Nick settled back down beside her.

'What happened then?'

'There was some confusion because Mr Nazar accused her of stealing and she was shouting that he had threatened her. Inspector Western had somehow taken control of her shopping bag and said that he would search it, with her permission. She agreed and he then found the cans of meat. She went barmy and Mr Nazar started shouting.'

'So the shopkeeper planted the cans?' he asked.

'He never went near the bag, Nick.'

'You're absolutely certain that when you carried it back to the shop it was empty?' he asked.

'It did not contain twelve cans of meat.'

'So who put them in the bag, Sarah?'

***

PC Rudd was uncomfortable. She was regretting her decision to ask to see Inspector Western. She had passed a sleepless night, some of which had been spent feeding Marcus. She had talked through her problems with him, but her son had seemed more focused on his stomach and had had nothing useful to say. Nick had snored the hours away.

'Yes, PC Rudd. I'm busy. What is it?' Inspector Western looked up from his paperwork.

'I think that Mr Nazar planted the cans of meat yesterday, sir.'

'Pardon?'

Sarah recounted the arrest that had taken place and went through the series of events that had led Inspector Western to find the cans of meat in the bag.

Inspector Western put down his pen and sighed.

'Mr Nazar never went near the bag,' he said. 'I asked to look into it. She agreed. I found the cans. End of story.'

'She said that she did not take the cans, sir, and when I carried the bag back to the shop, it was empty.'

'You made a mistake, PC Rudd.'

'With respect, sir, there were no cans of meat in the bag that I carried back to the shop.'

'So, it was Mr Nazar planted them. Does it matter? That woman is a serial shoplifter. I could smell it a mile away. She'll be fined and then go and rob another shop. Go away, PC Rudd.'

As she left his office, she felt her stomach tightening.

'But you said that all our citizens are equal, you two-faced hypocrite,' she said to herself under her breath.

***

Her shift was over at two o'clock and she was due to begin a four-day break. She changed in the locker room and put on her coat: it was getting colder. She then walked the two miles to the housing estate. Despite the poor street lighting, she found the property and knocked on the door. The rubbish was spilling out of the dustbin and there was a partly dismantled motorbike on the lawn. The sound of crying was coming from inside.

The shoplifter opened the door and immediately recognised her visitor.

'Oh, you're the copper from yesterday. It's late. Fuck off!'

Sarah managed to gain entry and arrived in a kitchen which, to her surprise, was clean and tidy.

'Only the baby's here at the moment. The other three are at school. Dave's at work and he'll be going to the pub later.'

'I suppose he has to relax,' said Sarah.

'To fucking work! We've got fucking debts but we're getting there. For the first time I have a chance to provide for my girls properly.'

They had a coffee together and Sarah told her about Marcus.

'I want a boy,' she said.

'From what I saw yesterday, you can't provide properly for any more children,' said PC Rudd.

'Why are you here, copper?'

Sarah became distracted and then muddled and then she blurted out that she knew that the cans had been planted in her bag and she knew who had done it.

'Well, Sherlock Holmes, you've got that fucking wrong.'

'But the bag was empty when I carried it back to the shop.'

'I'd thieved nothing, copper. That fucking Asian accused me of shoplifting when I was innocent. So I thought to myself 'fuck you!' and when your police mate was making a big fuss in the shop I put the cans in the bag.'

She walked round the table and poured herself a glass of vodka.

'Then he wanted to look inside it and I'd no bleedin' choice but to agree. But don't you fret. The courts are on my side. I'll get off. After all, I didn't do nothing wrong, did I? And how the fuck am I supposed to put food on the table for my kiddies without a bit of snitchin'?'

As Sarah left the house, even more depressed than when she'd entered, she felt herself being pulled back by her coat.

'Eh, copper, how do you think the world works, then? It's dog eat dog, innit?'

***

Inspector Western looked up as Sarah sat down in front of him. She had used her time off to spring clean the house, play with her son and make her husband some wholesome evening meals. On the final day, she was informed that she must see her boss the following day at 8.00 a.m.

'So? What did she say?' he asked.

'Who? What are we talking about, sir?'

'One of our patrol cars saw you on the housing estate. You visited the woman we did for shoplifting. You were in plain clothes. I hope you did not say you were there on official business, Police Constable Rudd.'

'I didn't say much at all, sir. She did all the talking.'

'So?'

'She planted the cans in her own bag, sir. She thought she might get away with it.'

'I know that, PC Rudd. I saw her do it.'

Sarah looked at him in amazement.

'You spotted it?' she asked.

'That's why I asked to search her bag. I knew they were in there.'

'But...'

'But nothing. She shot herself in the foot. She had, at that point, not committed an offence. She'd not left the shop. But I knew that she could not say what had happened. She had no choice but to play along with it.'

'But she was innocent, sir.'

'She intended leaving the shop with twelve cans of meat for which she had not paid.'

'But…'

'PC Rudd,' he shouted. 'What about Mr Nazar? He's being robbed all the time. Thugs held him up late at night.'

'Oh, I see, sir. The end justifies the means.'

'Would she have left the shop with the cans?'

'We don't know, sir.'

'Well, I do know. I have the streets of Stevenage to think about and my job is to reassure our people that they are safe.'

Sarah's head sank down to her chest

'She said that she has to shoplift to provide for her children.'

'They all say that, PC Rudd. Was there a television, a washing machine, clothes and the rest? Did her children seem hungry?'

'They were at school, sir.' She paused. 'She told us that her partner has a second job to try to make ends meet.'

'Did they go on holiday to Spain by any chance?'

'I've no way of knowing that, sir.'

'She was cautioned at Luton airport in July. She'd lifted items of clothing from one of the shops. They decided not to prosecute and she flew off to the sun with her children. Let's just say this was just a bit of redressing the balance, shall we? She didn't get done in Luton, though she was caught fair and square, but we did arrest her last week for something that she hadn't yet done, but was clearly going to do.'

'Can I go, please, sir?'

'You'll go through your career having to make difficult decisions, Sarah.'

'Thank you, sir.'

As she went down the stairs to the ground floor, she muttered some words to herself.

'You fucking bastard!' seemed to sum up her feelings nicely.

***

Hurricane Sarah hit the Rudd household later that evening: Nick took the full force as she unleashed her anger.

Her stormy rhetoric centred on what she felt was an abuse of his authority by Inspector Western. More than an abuse: how the hell could it be right to arrest somebody for something they were going to do, if they hadn't actually done it?

'He was totally judgemental, Nick. He justified what he did because he dismissed her as a human being, as a citizen of our society, all because he wanted to reassure Mr Nazar.'

'He's under pressure from his bosses over the race issue, is my guess, Sarah.'

'And that justifies everything does it, Nick?'

He paused and looked out of the window.

'Give me an answer, please,' she pleaded.

'I can't. These conundrums disturb us all.' He paused. 'But I'll tell you one thing. My experience is that if you dig deep enough, there is good in everybody.'

She moved over and grabbed Nick by the lapels of his jacket.

'And that's what you truly believe, is it, Nick?'

He hesitated. 'In the end, Sarah, justice will prevail. Somewhere, out there, is some fairness.'

***

She tossed and she turned and she hurt. At six o'clock the next morning she decided that either Inspector Western needed to agree to withdraw the charge of shoplifting or she'd resign from the force. She arrived outside his office at seven fifty-two. She knocked on the door. It swung open in front of her. She walked in.

The desk was empty with just a blotting paper pad and a pen remaining.

She heard a noise behind her and turned to face Chief Superintendent Marian Musgrove.

'PC Rudd, how can I help you?'

'Oh, ma'am. Good morning, ma'am.' Her voice faltered. 'I was expecting to speak to Inspector Western.'

'Speak about what?'

'Nothing really, ma'am.'

'Do you normally visit the Inspector's office to talk about nothing, PC Rudd?'

Sarah hesitated. She wished she'd let matters be.

'There was an incident a few days ago, ma'am. I merely wanted to clarify something.'

'That will not be possible.'

'Ma'am?'

'Inspector Western is away on sick leave and will not be returning to this station.'

Sarah paused. 'Well, he looked as fit as a fiddle the last time I saw him.'

Chief Superintendent Musgrove sighed. She closed the door behind them both and indicated that Sarah should sit down.

'This goes no further. Do we understand each other, PC Rudd?'

'Yes, ma'am. No further.'

'The move of Inspector Western to this force was no accident. There had been some suggestions. We were watching.'

'For what?'

'That doesn't matter. I regret to say that there has been a further, shall we say, incident.'

'I need to know, ma'am.'

CS Musgrove looked intently at the police officer who reminded her of herself, twenty years earlier. She knew that she should not be discussing the allegations.

'Inspector Western is suspected of, shall we say, cooking the books. There have been more charges brought on rather more flimsy grounds than seems entirely healthy. It appears that Inspector Western's passion for positive statistics might have led him to twist the facts on more than one occasion.' She hesitated again. 'For your ears only, PC Rudd.' The Chief Superintendent paused. 'Inspector Western is facing disciplinary procedures, and is not likely to be on the force much longer, if I have any say in the matter.'

Sarah felt her body relax. She stood up to resume her duties.

'Understood, ma'am. Matter closed,' she said as she left the office.

***

Her day on the streets of Stevenage followed a normal routine. Two women in 4x4s clashed in the Tesco car park over the one remaining space. There were three episodes of shoplifting. A junkie had to be arrested in a doctor's surgery. A cyclist and a bus driver had an argument which closed a street.

She arrived back at the police station at four o'clock. Tonight was going to be a special evening for Nick. She smiled to herself as she prepared to sign off.

The Duty Sergeant called her over. 'Sarah, there's a woman asking for you.'

She headed for the interview room. 'No,' said the Sergeant, 'she's outside. She wouldn't stay here and wait for you.'

As Sarah exited through the main entrance, she saw to her left the woman who'd been accused of shoplifting. Alongside her were three small girls. As she approached them, each came up to her and gave her a small bunch of flowers, which had been stolen from the local cemetery earlier in the day. Had she been able to check, two of the daughters had holes in their shoes. Their dinner that night was going to be off-cuts from the butcher and boiled potatoes.

She stood in front of the woman.

'You came to see me. I was out of order to say what I said. We want to tell you, we're sorry.'

'I'll see what I can do about the charges against you,' said Sarah.

'Been dropped. Copper came to see me yesterday.' She turned back. 'But I'd have got off, anyway,' she laughed, as the girls joined hands and skipped away together.

***

Nick looked at Sarah as she stepped through the front door.

'Who gave you the flowers?' he asked.

Sarah removed her jacket and started unbuttoning her shirt.

'If you dig deep enough, Nick, there's good in everybody.'

THE CHOCOLATE SCREEN

February, 2001

PC 8377 Sarah Rudd threw off the bed-covers, kissed her sleeping husband, checked the baby monitor and took off her nightshirt. She stood in front of the full-length mirror and examined her curves. Everything looked to be in rather good shape. She ran her fingers through her hair and held her hands on top of her scalp.

The right part of the human brain is associated with creativity. It is a word which is not entirely synonymous with, but nor was it very far away from the noun 'intuition', which derives from the Latin verb *intueor*, which means 'to look closely'. Another related word is 'perception', but is that the same as instinct?

At the end of the day that lay ahead, Sarah Rudd would have a better understanding of the importance of a police officer's intuition. The learning curve would be both dangerous and painful.

***

He looked down at the news summary from his morning paper:

A Scottish Court in the Netherlands has convicted a Libyan and acquitted another for their part in the bombing of Pan Am Flight 103 which crashed in

Lockerbie in 1988. Al Amin Khalifah Fhimah (aged 44) has been cleared, but Abdelbaset Ali Mohamed al-Megrahi has been found guilty and sentenced to life imprisonment, with a recommended minimum term of twenty years.

He groaned inwardly, but it wasn't the length of the sentence that was the cause of his dismay. He had sighted the colleague who was joining him for his morning's work.

She opened the passenger door and immediately expressed exaggerated pleasure at seeing her companion.

'Detective Constable Rodney Windsor!' exclaimed PC Rudd. 'What a lovely surprise!'

'Who for?' he asked.

She settled into her seat, having thrown her coat into the back of his car. 'And how is the lovely Lady Jane Windsor?' she teased.

'Her name's Vanessa.'

'Lovely name. Let me guess… Lady Vanessa Coutts-Rothschild.'

'Vanessa Reynolds.' He paused. 'Let me ask you a question, PC Rudd. What's the connection between Abdelbaset Ali Mohammed al-Megrahi and myself?'

Sarah pretended to give his question serious thought. 'I'll have to pass on that one,' she said.

'We both feel as though we've been given life sentences.'

'I'm only with you for a week!' she exclaimed as she read the newspaper article he handed her.

'Exactly,' said DC Windsor.

'Come on, Rodders,' she laughed. 'Let's go and save the world. It will do your career no end of good.'

They left the security of the station car park and

drove out of the town until they reached a farm on the western side of the A1(M). DC Windsor turned in and reduced his speed over the potholes. They eventually reached a group of buildings: several of the sheds were in a state of disrepair.

'Stay here,' he ordered his companion.

He disappeared into the first shed and came out four minutes later.

'He won't cooperate. I'll have to get a warrant.'

'What are you looking for?' asked PC Rudd.

He handed her a fact sheet issued by the Ministry of Agriculture. 'Read this.'

'A pesticide is a chemical or biological agent (such as a virus, bacterium, antimicrobial, or disinfectant) that deters, incapacitates, kills, or otherwise discourages pests. Target pests can include insects, plant pathogens, weeds, molluscs, birds, mammals, fish, nematodes (roundworms), and microbes that destroy property, cause nuisance, or spread disease, or are disease vectors. Although pesticides have benefits, some also have drawbacks, such as potential toxicity to humans and other desired species. According to the Stockholm Convention on Persistent Organic Pollutants, nine of the twelve most dangerous and persistent organic chemicals are pesticides…

'It's fascinating, Rodney.'

'Carry on reading.'

Sarah looked at the next heading on the sheet:

'Carbamates: Carbamate pesticides feature the carbamate ester functional group. Included in this group are aldicarb (Temik), carbofuran (Furadan), carbaryl (Sevin), ethienocarb, fenobucarb, oxamyl and methomyl. These chemicals kill insects by reversibly inactivating the enzyme acetylcholinesterase. The organophosphate pesticides also inhibit this enzyme, although irreversibly, and cause a more severe form of cholinergic poisoning. Fenoxycarb has a carbamate group but acts as a juvenile hormone mimic, rather than inactivating acetylcholinesterase. The insect repellent icaridin is a substituted carbamate.

'Rodney, can we go and arrest some speeding motorists, please?'

'That's Traffic. I'm a detective.'

'So what happens now?'

'Read the last sentence again, Sarah. This is about icaridin. There is a rogue supply being distributed and the hospital has called us in. They've had three cases of severe skin burns. All are foreign workers. If it reaches the lungs it can be fatal. I'm trying to find the supplier.'

'So why are we here?'

'We received an anonymous phone call pointing a finger at this farm.'

'Why didn't you say that? This is a case for PC Sarah Rudd.'

DC Windsor groaned. Sarah told him to hand her the sheets again. She spent some minutes absorbing the information.

'Icaridin, here I come,' she announced as she got out of the car. 'Stay here, Rodney, and dream about Vanessa.'

Seventeen minutes later, she returned to the vehicle and instructed her fellow officer to drive away. As they turned onto the main road, he asked her for an explanation.

'It's coming from Grange Farm, two miles south. The farmer is called Edmund Flynn. He's bringing it in from Ireland. You'll need a warrant, Rodney.'

'So how did you ascertain that?' snapped the frustrated police officer.

'The uniform, Rodney. You detectives forget that it can influence people. I told our friendly farmer that I'm attached to Special Branch and I could smell the icaridin. I used several long words. I told him that Fenoxycarb was a chemical substitute with excessive hormones and I suspected that methomyl was involved.'

'But that's nonsense.'

'Of course it is! I said that, provided he agreed to tell me who the supplier is, we might not come back.'

'You'll never get away with that, Sarah.'

'Turnip head doesn't know that, does he?' she said.

DC Windsor snorted. 'You were lucky. You put yourself in a position of danger.'

'Well, Rodney, I'm only a weak, impetuous woman, and a PC as well. How could I know any better?'

'Yes, you should leave the detective work to me. Where did you say the supplier is based?'

***

She had lost weight and was ecstatic. She could not quite tighten her belt to the target notch but she was almost there. Sarah Rudd was a woman who knew her body and understood exactly what it could achieve.

The canteen in Stevenage Police Station was full. Traffic was busy with the consequences of the icy roads and the officers were calling in for regular refreshments. Somebody was stealing lead off church buildings and the Public Protection Unit was dealing with several cases of stranger rape.

71

She put her tray down and gave him a special smile.

'Why, Detective Windsor, what a lovely surprise.'

She arranged her plate of eggs, bacon, tomatoes, black pudding and sausages in front of her and showered her breakfast with tomato ketchup.

'I've lost another couple of pounds. Does it show?' she teased.

DC Windsor groaned.

'Gosh, Rodney. Muesli and bran flakes, with fresh orange juice. What a healthy little boy you are.'

'Have you any idea what you are doing to your insides, PC Rudd?' He used his serviette to wipe his mouth, and drank some more green tea. 'You are soaking yourself with cholesterol, your arteries are furring up and you are jeopardising your longevity.'

Sarah laughed. 'I have an eight-month-old son who has kept me up all night, a demanding husband who insists I keep his home in apple-pie order, and, Detective Windsor, I am a full-time police officer who continually works extra hours because she cares.'

'Vanessa does that,' he said.

'Does what?'

'When you're cross, you pout your lips.'

Do I? thought Sarah. *Better check that out.*

Out loud, she said, 'Are there any other similarities between me and Lady Vanessa?'

'She's a research assistant at Cambridge University. Her speciality is South African history in the early nineteenth century. I helped her one night at the side of the main road: she'd broken down. We've been seeing each other ever since.' He paused. 'She's rather...'

Sarah buttered a third piece of toast and poured

him some more orange juice, nodding at a fellow officer who waved in her direction.

'She's rather what, Rodney?'

'I know she likes me, but she's said she can't see me this weekend. She's writing a paper on the influence of Shaka Zulu on the integration of the Zulu peoples, 1816–1828.'

Sarah decided to spread some more jam on her toast.

'She's a bundle of fun, isn't she? Have you told her how you feel about her?'

'Oh, I couldn't do that. I must wait for things to develop.'

Sarah drank her cup of tea. 'Do you know what I suggest you do, Rodney?'

'I think I'm about to find out,' he groaned.

'You should go up to Cambridge this weekend and surprise her. Put on your sexiest Zulu loincloth and show her what an assegai really can achieve... and don't forget the flowers.'

She looked up and saw that Chief Superintendent Marian Musgrove was standing at their table. She handed DC Windsor a piece of paper.

'We're short-staffed. Please go there now, both of you. Neighbour says there was a child screaming during the night. Her name is written on the bottom. For some reason, I've only just received this message'

'I'm not right for this, ma'am,' stuttered DC Windsor.

'You'll have PC Rudd with you,' snapped Chief Superintendent Musgrove.

They were silent in the car. DC Windsor parked the vehicle and reported in to base.

'DC Windsor with PC Rudd. We're on scene and

dealing.'

They walked together up the pathway slipping on the untreated frozen snow.

'You take the lead, Rodney,' said Sarah.

He pressed the bell, which did not work. He knocked on the door and, after a few moments, an unshaven man answered.

'I'm Detective Constable Windsor and this is PC Rudd. We've had reports of a child screaming.'

The man looked towards the house on his left. 'I'll fucking sort him out this time, nosey bastard!'

'May we come in, please?'

'No.'

'Your name, please, sir?'

'Eddy Taylor. You're not coming in.'

He's playing for time, Sarah thought to herself.

'You need to understand that I'm ex-SAS.'

'We are coming in, Mr Taylor,' and much to Sarah's surprise, DC Windsor pushed straight past him. She followed quickly.

The hallway contained a colourful carpet on which there were a number of boxes. Sarah lifted a lid and saw that there were piles of DVDs inside it.

Rodney had now reached the kitchen, where he found a woman holding a baby. Sitting to her right was a girl of about two years old who was wearing a Winnie the Pooh nightdress. She was spreading chocolate over her face.

'Lolita, you silly girl,' laughed the mother. She turned to the police officers. 'She so loves her chocolate.'

'For breakfast?' exclaimed Sarah.

'My Meg's a great mother. She looks after Lolly and George bloody well,' said the former Special

Forces soldier.

'We mustn't keep you from your work, Mr Taylor,' said DC Windsor.

'On the sick, mate. Took a bullet in the chest, year before last. I was part of the Kosovo Verification Mission. Needed to drop a couple of Serb top brass. We misjudged their protection.' He coughed painfully. 'I now wholesale war films. Quite a market out there. The older guys want to relive their adventures.'

Sarah was looking around: the kitchen was immaculate. The draining board was sparkling from a recent clean. The electric stove was clear and there was no washing-up in sight.

'May I please have your permission to look at the children's bedrooms?' she asked.

'No,' said Eddy Taylor.

'Oh, go on Eddy. I want to put George down for a sleep,' said Meg Taylor.

'You can see his room,' said the father. He took Sarah upstairs. The carpets were freshly hoovered. The small bedroom was populated by cartoon characters. Sarah could smell disinfectant.

They returned to the lounge. There was no shortage of family purchases, with a twenty-six-inch TV, computers and personal stereos.

'Thank you for your time, Mr Taylor,' said DC Windsor.

Sarah looked daggers at him but followed slowly as they left the property. They both sat back in the car.

'Well, Rodney, you fucked up there.'

'Shut up, Sarah! There was nothing for us: two parents; two children; immaculate house; no shortage of money. The neighbour got it wrong.'

'Let's go and ask him.' She paused. 'Where's the piece of paper that CS Musgrove gave you?' She took it out of Rodney's outstretched hand.

'Mrs Petrov. Sounds like the wife of an exiled Serbian General,' laughed Sarah.

The property was situated in a corner position and they were able to drive the police car out of sight and reach a side door on which they knocked. Mrs Petrov came out and told them that her husband did not speak English. She confirmed that she had phoned the police this morning after Mr Petrov had told her that he'd heard a child screaming in the night. She was able to confirm that the time was around five-thirty. She also said that it was not the first time they had heard these sounds. Their house was rather dark and untidy.

DC Windsor and PC Rudd stood outside and mused together.

'One tidy house; one tip. Strange old world.' He paused. 'I should have asked Mr Taylor to let me have a look in those boxes: probably porn.'

'Look no further,' said DC Rudd holding up a DVD.

DC Windsor looked at the cover: it was *A Bridge Too Far* which had been made in 1977. It told the Second World War story of how, in 1944, the Allies had attempted to shorten the ending of the hostilities by breaking through the German defences in the Netherlands. The key strategy was that they had to take several river crossings including the Arnhem Bridge: it had proved to be one too many.

'That's that,' he said.

'Have you got your PC in the car?' asked Sarah. 'He might be pulling the oldest trick in the book. We need to know what's on that disc.'

They returned to the vehicle and DC Windsor was soon looking at the DVD, and at the opening scenes of *A Bridge Too Far*: it proved to be the whole film.

Sarah sat back in her seat and frowned.

'Rodney, the Taylors' house, was everything immaculate?'

'Pretty much. Rather impressive, I thought.'

'Everything, Rodney?' She looked out of the window. 'And do you think the Petrovs would naturally mislead us?'

'You're grasping at straws, Sarah.'

'We're going back in,' she said. 'Do you give a young child chocolate for her breakfast?'

'We're not, Sarah. We'll be breaking our orders,' he gasped as he chased after her up the path.

They arrived at the front door and Sarah stood to one side. She pointed to where she wanted her colleague to stand.

'Bang loudly and then grab him,' ordered Sarah.

The door was answered almost immediately. Mr Taylor was propelled out as DC Windsor held on to his jacket and yanked him forwards.

Sarah rushed in and went straight up the stairs. She opened the door opposite the bedroom occupied by the baby. Lolita was lying naked on the covers. There was a camera positioned at the bottom of the bed. She was sobbing quietly. Sarah grabbed for her handkerchief and wiped the chocolate off her face. It was a mass of bruises and there was a tooth missing. She held her in her arms and went out to the landing.

Eddy Taylor had succeeded in returning to the hallway, where DC Windsor was struggling to hold on to his legs. The father turned and kicked him in the face.

Sarah had her radio to her mouth.

'PC Rudd. Officer down. Urgent help needed.'

Rodney, again, tried in vain to halt the progress of Eddy Taylor, only to receive a lashing to his stomach. He curled up in agony.

The ex-SAS veteran reached almost to the top of the stairs, where he slipped and fell to his knees: he looked up and found Sarah holding the child and staring down at him.

'One more step towards me and I'll kill you,' she said.

He looked into her eyes and initially backed down. This gave Sarah the chance to kick out and she caught him high on his forehead. He fell backwards and landed by the prostrate body of DC Windsor.

The early morning peace was shattered by the sound of multiple sirens as more police officers arrived on the scene. Paramedics reached DC Windsor while Eddy Taylor was handcuffed and taken away.

Sarah walked slowly down the stairs and into the kitchen where Meg Taylor was holding baby George.

'He made me do it,' she pleaded.

Sarah looked at her with total contempt. She then realised that Lolita was being taken off her.

'I'm a doctor,' said a voice.

She watched as the child was taken away for medical help and then to begin a new life, with her brother George, in a foster home. She reached the bottom of the path just as DC Windsor was stretchered into the ambulance.

Sarah walked away, seeking some solitude. She wandered down the street, impervious to the cold morning air. She was upset and she was very angry.

She breathed in deeply and shook with frustration.

'Never again,' she chided herself, 'will I ever overlook the obvious.'

'Intuition': from the Latin *intueor* 'to look closely.'

***

Two weeks later, Sarah Rudd was frustrated. She had put on two pounds in weight and had to stretch her belt to another notch. She was celebrating this defeat with fish and chips and an extra portion of pease pudding. She looked up in surprise. There, in front of her, was a colleague.

'DC Windsor,' she cried. 'What a lovely surprise. You've recovered quickly.'

'I've come to say goodbye,' he said.

'But we're just getting to know each other,' she laughed.

'I'm transferring to Cambridge. To be honest, I think there's a bit of a promotion involved.'

'And what else might attract you to our university town, Rodders?'

'Funny you should ask, Sarah. I'm moving in with Vanessa.'

He held out his hand and she took it. She wondered about kissing him, but decided against it. He moved away and then turned round. He handed her a package. It was about fifteen inches long.

'This is for you,' he said and then he was gone.

She sat down and sighed. She'd miss Rodders. She undid the wrapping and found inside a small spear wrapped in coarse brown paper. She opened it out and started to read the immaculate handwriting:

The word 'assegai' is Arabic for 'spear'. The Zulu warrior Shaka designed a shorter version, as enclosed, which was called the 'iklwa'. This was the sound it made as it was being withdrawn from the victim's wound. The 'assegai' has been known to be used for a range of purposes. Love, Vanessa x

As she stepped out on to the streets of Stevenage, Sarah smiled to herself.

She was thinking of what her husband Nick would look like brandishing his *iklwa*…

ALL BUYERS ARE LIARS.

November, 2001

'Please talk sense. What do you mean, 150 over 95? I sell kitchen systems. I'm moving to a new company on the Stevenage Trading Estate. I'm told I must have a medical examination and now I'm referred back to my doctor. I still play rugby, I'm fit… and now I'm ill?'

Dr Liz Hancock groaned. The allocated ten minutes for her surgery time with Jason Samuels was under pressure and she had a maternity clinic to run.

'Mr Samuels,' she said, 'you have hypertension. We know that from your blood pressure results. I checked you when you came in, and again, just now. The reading has, in fact, gone up.'

'To what?'

'156 over 97.'

'Meaning what?'

'Right, Mr Samuels, we are talking about the blood pressure in your body. The first figure we call the systolic reading and this measures the pressure in your arteries as the heart contracts. It should be around 120. The second is the diastolic and is the pressure as your heart relaxes. We like to see a figure of 80.'

'If I tried to sell my kitchen units using this language, I'd be sacked!' he laughed.

'Mr Samuels, I'm taking this seriously. I suggest you do.' Dr Hancock sat back and put the testing equipment away. 'First of all, we have to decide whether you are simply hypertensive or whether there is an underlying cause.'

'Which is what?'

'You're not taking any prescriptive medicines so it can be obesity, kidney problems, even sleeping disorders. I'm going to take a blood test which hopefully will eliminate anything serious. Then we'll decide which drug is best for you. Blood pressure is fickle, but if the readings don't reduce I may put you on, what we call, *ambulatory monitoring*: we strap a little machine to you and it takes a reading every thirty minutes.'

'Do I wear it in the scrum?' he laughed.

'Please roll up your sleeve,' said the doctor as she prepared to take a blood sample. She then asked him to stand on the weighing scales. She noted the reading and consulted her tables.

'You are six foot two inches tall, and are probably about thirty pounds over your optimum weight level.'

'You should see the size of the prop I played against last Saturday,' he replied. 'Heavy bastard, he was.'

As her patient left the surgery, she asked him to come back if, at any time, he felt unwell. He turned round and faced her.

'There's one thing you can't cure, doctor,' he said, 'a wife who wants to buy a house that we can't fucking afford.'

***

Detective Constable Sarah Rudd was frustrated. Two months earlier she had successfully applied to join the

CID. She'd had enough of patrolling the streets of Stevenage, and wanted some more interesting action. She was determined to arrest the bad guys.

This particular weekday had started badly. Marcus, now seventeen months old, had developed spots overnight and husband Nick was none too pleased to be delegated the trip to the medical centre. He was also seething at his school's latest Ofsted report following their recent visit. The family's financial resources were being drained by the cost of full-time child care, and he and Sarah were not as harmonious as they had been.

DC Rudd had been assigned to the case of disappearing 'For Sale' boards. Several local estate agents were reporting the theft of their equipment from outside clients' houses. Uniform Division was keeping a watchful observation in the expectation that local youths were having some fun. They had not, as yet, apprehended anyone.

Detective Sergeant Simon Trimble was having no truck with her moans as he listened to her protests.

'That's for the foot soldiers, sir. I'm a detective,' she protested.

'Then go and solve a crime, DC Rudd.' He picked up a file from his desk. It was labelled 'G. Freeman'. He handed it to her. 'Here's a clue,' he chuckled.

She decamped to the canteen and decided that her diet would start again on the following Monday. She poured HP sauce over the sausages and hash browns and added an extra helping of sugar to her mug of tea, as she started to study the folder in front of her and became interested in the case of the disappearing estate agents' boards.

An hour later, and despite the inner comfort of her

cholesterol-laden breakfast, Sarah was now shivering in the chilly, early morning, November winds. She tried humming the words of Michael Jackson's latest album number: *'why ain't you feelin' me, she's invincible. But I can do anything, she's invincible.'*

She was watching the rear premises of a High Street estate agent's business, hoping that a van would arrive loaded with 'For Sale' boards displaying the names of rival firms.

DS Trimble's file had given her a useful insight into the background of the proprietor, Gary Freeman. He had form. He had set up Premium House Sales fifteen months earlier, following a six-month period on probation, after he had been convicted of falsely obtaining supplier credit for his van hire business, using doctored accounts and dodgy references. He was considered fortunate not to go to prison, but a key witness had made a last-minute decision not to give evidence against him.

He was now proving successful in obtaining selling instructions and finding buyers. There were rumours and suspicions amongst other agents that he was undervaluing properties and selling them to his associates who sold them on, some months later, and split the profits with him. The police needed a complaint from a vendor on which they could act, but people dealing with Gary Freeman seemed unwilling to become involved.

Sarah watched the rear of the property until nine o'clock, when she returned to the police station for a coffee. Thirty minutes later, she returned to the offices of Premium House sales and walked into a row between two men.

'You fucking promised me that I could buy it for

£92,500,' yelled Jason Samuels. 'Give me my fucking grand back, you shit!'

'Careful with your words,' cautioned Gary Freeman. 'I might get cross with you.'

'You and whose army, shitface?'

DC Rudd coughed and held up her warrant card.

'Detective Constable Rudd. Can I be of help?' she asked.

Jason looked at her, grimaced and rushed out of the office. Gary Freeman slumped down into his chair behind a dishevelled desk.

'What do you want?' he snapped.

'I'm looking into the disappearance of some agent's sale boards, Mr Freeman. Do you know anything about it?'

He looked at her with a certain disdain. 'Yes, love. Several of mine have gone missing. Kids, I suppose. I've simply replaced them. Investigating a crimewave are we?'

He lit up a cigarette and blew the smoke towards her face. Sarah walked round the room and looked at some of the properties being advertised for sale.

'Are sales good, Mr Freeman?'

Before he could answer, she said that she and her husband were looking to sell.

'Mr Rudd wants four bedrooms,' she explained.

A young woman entered the office and took off her coat. Sarah ignored her as she went out to the back of the premises. There was nothing further to attract her attention.

'What was the name of the person who was in here?' she asked.

'Tony Blair.'

'I'll be back' she said as she left the building.

***

DC Rudd returned to her desk and checked out three

car registration numbers she had noted outside the offices of Premium House Sales. She was banking on the Ford Mondeo belonging to the visitor to the premises. The first of the vehicles did not show up; the second belonged to an owner living in Cornwall; and the third was registered to Swedish Fitted Kitchens. She visited the company on the Trading Estate and, to her surprise, found the car outside the reception area. Before long, she was together with Jason Samuels in a private room.

'Mr Samuels, you were in the offices of Premium House Sales earlier this morning.'

He looked at her. 'You were the copper who came in,' he said.

'Correct. You were having an argument with Mr Freeman.'

He laughed. 'No, he's trying to find me a house that I can afford.'

'You wanted your money back. That's what I heard,' said DC Rudd.

'No, no. I'd put a grand down to secure a three-bedroom place in Granville Road. My missus is desperate to move. I'd told her we'd got it, but Mr Freeman said he'd had a higher offer. Fair play. We lost it.'

'You seemed rather angry, Mr Samuels.'

'Have you met my missus?'

'What was the address of the property?'

Jason Samuels stood up. 'I've had enough of this. I've not made a complaint. You're out of order.'

He stormed out of the room. It was just as well that he was due to return to see his doctor in the evening for a blood pressure check.

***

DC Rudd knew where Granville Road was and reached the area within ten minutes. She parked her car and walked slowly up and down looking for an estate agent's board. Towards the end of the street, she spotted a sign lying on the grass inside the front garden of a three bedroom semi-detached home built, she estimated, twenty years earlier.

She knocked on the front door. She identified herself to an elderly woman who read her warrant card and said that she could come in. Her offer to make a cup of tea was immediately accepted and before long they were sharing a packet of bourbon biscuits.

Mrs Elsie Williams was a willing talker. She told Sarah that her husband was in bed with severe leg pains and the doctor was due to visit in the afternoon. They did not want to move from their home, but a man had called to tell them there was a planned road-widening scheme to allow buses to use the route to the town. They could lose some of their front garden. He had offered to sell their house before the news broke. She was surprised at the suggested price of £90,000 because one down the street had fetched more, but he'd pointed out the poor condition of the property.

'Can you remember his name, Elsie?' asked DC Rudd.

'Mr Freeman. Yes, Mr Freeman. A nice man. He told Alfie and me that he'd served in the army and taken part of the rescue of our soldiers in Sierra Leone. I remember seeing it on the telly.'

'So he introduced Mr Samuels to you?'

'No, it didn't happen that way. More tea, dear?'

Sarah watched as she disappeared into the kitchen. They were soon chatting away together.

'Mr Freeman was slow to have a 'For Sale' board

put up and Alfred, that's him upstairs, wanted one. He was in the army and he's very correct about things.' She hurriedly drank her tea. 'One day, Mr Samuels arrived with his wife and before I knew what was happening he came back and said they were buying the house. He wouldn't say how much he was paying for it.'

Mrs Williams began to get upset and Sarah suggested that she'd return to see her on another day.

'You stay where you are. May I call you Susan?'

'I'd prefer Sarah,' she laughed, 'but of course you can.' She drank some more tea and helped herself to another biscuit.

'So what happened then, Mrs Williams?'

'It's Elsie. Everybody calls me that. Mr Samuels came back and shouted that we'd sold it to somebody else. He was very cross. I told him that I didn't know what he was talking about. Alfred tried to get downstairs, but his legs gave way. It was like a mad house, Susan.'

***

Jason Samuels left the surgery and reread the appointment card. Dr Hancock was so concerned about his blood pressure readings that she'd arranged for him to have tests at the local hospital. He tore the card into small pieces and threw them away. He knew better than she did what was causing a result of 168/102. He was not to know that it was the second figure, the diastolic reading, which was worrying his doctor. He decided to call in at the rugby club for a beer and then go home for the inevitable row with his wife.

***

The casualty doctor adjusted the oxygen mask over

the face of his patient. He had satisfied himself that the three broken ribs had not penetrated his lungs after studying the X-rays. He looked again at the damage to his face: it was the blow to the right eye that was the real concern and he was relieved that the consultant ophthalmologist was on his way to assess the damage.

'Doctor Baines, the police want to speak to you,' said the nurse.

Detective Sergeant Trimble thanked him for his time. He argued that he must speak to the victim but was told that was simply not possible.

***

Nick closed the door behind him so Sarah could have a private telephone conversation. She soon returned back to him.

'That was the boss,' said Sarah as they settled back into their lounge.

'It's unusual for him to phone here,' said Nick.

'You know I can't tell you about police matters,' she said.

She pretended to resist his promptings in the hopes of securing some affection: she'd give in easily. He poured her a decent sized gin and tonic and fifteen minutes later, his wife was relating the story of the missing estate agents' boards.

'Come on,' chided Nick. 'There's no way that your boss would call to discuss that.'

Sarah swallowed and asked for a refill.

'An estate agent has been beaten up and is in hospital. The main possibility is the man I interviewed this morning. DS Trimble wanted to know the details.'

'Case closed. Let's talk about our finances.'

'Case wide open, Nick. At the time of the assault, the suspect was in the police station being charged with drink-driving.'

'Sounds as though he's got lots of enemies, this estate agent.'

'Who'd risk beating him up? I don't think so.'

'We're overdrawn at the bank, Sarah. We must cut back.'

'On what?'

'Food?'

'At least you didn't raise the cost of childcare, Nick.'

He drank deeply and frowned. 'We paid too much for this house, Sarah. Our mortgage payments are crippling us. We'll have to sell up.'

'And get what for it?' she asked.

'£115,000 perhaps.'

'It's not worth more than £95,000. We both know that.'

'We'll say it's in magnificent condition.' He paused. 'All buyers are liars,' laughed Nick.

'Pardon?'

'A golfing pal used the term the other day. He'd been gazumped on a house purchase. The vendor gave his word that he'd sell it to him and then took a higher offer.'

'The buyer is the person who buys the house, Nick. It's a silly thing to say.' She frowned. "All sellers are liars' doesn't rhyme.'

Nick stood up and undid the buttons of his shirt.

'There's always one thing that doesn't cost money,' he suggested.

An hour later, Sarah lay on her back in bed and went over, once more, the day's events.

'All buyers are liars,' she said to herself.

***

The following morning, after learning that there was no improvement in the condition of Gary Freeman and that it was probable that he would need eye surgery, Sarah visited a local solicitor. She knew the receptionist, as a result of meeting her at the childcare clinic. Before long, she was in the office of the senior partner.

'I can only give you five minutes, DC Rudd, and I'll not discuss any client with you.'

Twenty minutes later, she left the offices with the knowledge that the solicitor was not aware of any road-widening scheme in Granville Road. He was not able to comment on the proposed bus route and suggested that she spoke to the Council on that one. He was more helpful with two recent sales of properties in the street, both of which had completed at prices over £110,000.

***

That evening Sarah relaxed with Nick after Marcus had taken an unusually long time to go to sleep.

'So how's the case of the vanishing estate agent boards?' he laughed.

She snuggled up to him. 'We're not selling this house, Nick. It's our home.'

'Can we fit the bank manager into the spare room?'

'Kinky thoughts now, Mr Rudd. Three in a bed, is it?'

'Now there's a thought. Have I told you about the new PE teacher? She played hockey for Australia. You should see her thighs.'

Sarah pretended to slap his face. 'What's her name?'

'Imogen. And they are tanned as well.'

'What are?'

'Her legs.'

Later that evening, Nick was snoring away, dreaming of Antipodean beauties, when he found himself woken up with a pot of tea.

'I don't want a cup,' he moaned. 'Leave me alone.'

'I want to talk,' said Sarah.

'What about?'

'Who beat up the estate agent?'

Nick sat up in bed. 'It was the bloke you interviewed. Good night, Sarah.'

But she'd had the same thought and had checked very carefully. Gary Freemen had been found at the back of his offices, lying on the ground, with blood pouring out of his face. The person making the 999 call was certain of the time and it was corroborated by the emergency services and the hospital. She had checked again and ten minutes earlier, Jason Samuels had been booked in at the police station. One of the officers had told her he was so drunk that he couldn't have hit Mr Blobby.

Sarah had laughed. She and Nick had never missed *Noel's House Party* on the television when it'd been on.

Nick suddenly sat up in bed.

'The obvious answer is that one of his enemies caught up with him and beat him up.' He paused. 'But that's too much of a coincidence for me, Sarah.'

'So who did it?' she mused. She checked the monitor and saw that Marcus was sleeping peacefully.

'All buyers are liars,' she said to herself, but she did not sleep easily as she decided to revisit all the events over the last two days. Instead, she tossed and turned as she tried to make sense of something that had been said to her.

***

She reported to DS Trimble the following morning. He was preoccupied with an attempted bank robbery which had taken place the previous day.

'Do what you can, Sarah,' he had said, and asked her to report back to him that evening.

She went back to her desk and reread her notes. She suddenly had an idea and looked up the address of the Army Recruitment Office in the High Street. An hour later, after an interesting chat with Sergeant Martin Weaver, she had her suspicions confirmed.

Sarah drove over to Granville Road and knocked on the door of a house. This time, Elsie Williams was not so pleased to see her and it took several minutes before she agreed to let her enter the house. After the inevitable cup of tea, Mrs Williams moaned that the doctor had been unable to help her husband, who was still in bed.

'I need to speak to him, please, Elsie,' said DC Rudd.

'Heavens, no! He's far too unwell.'

'Is he coming down or do I have to go upstairs to get him?'

'Alfie!' screamed Mrs Williams.

A bedroom door opened and Alfred Williams came out and stood at the top of the stairs staring down at DC Rudd.

'Okay, calm down, lass. I'm on my way.'

Sarah was hovering over her radio but decided to watch him as he came down the stairs and into the lounge.

Alfred Williams was a proud man who held himself erect.

'How did you guess?' he asked.

'Mr Williams, you're under arrest for causing grievous bodily harm to Gary Freeman. You do not have to say anything, but it may harm your defence if you do not mention when questioned something which you later rely on in court. Anything you do say may be given in evidence.'

Sarah paused.

'Do you understand what I am saying, Mr Williams?' She looked intensely at him. 'Is there anything you'd like to tell me?'

'As I said, how did you guess?'

'Gary Freeman was never in the army,' said Sarah.

'No, what he told us was utter garbage.'

'It was you who was lying, Mr Williams. You told Mrs Williams what to say.'

'So? You've proved nothing.'

'The British Army's operation in Sierra Leone was called Operation Pallister and began in May, 2000. Gary Freemen opened his offices around that time. You're an ex-services man. You would have known that he was lying.'

'He was a conman. He convinced us he would get us a good price. Jason Samuels was ready to pay £90,000. Then Freeman came back and said the price would be £85,000; that Jason Samuels had backed out, but he'd found another buyer. Then Jason called round and told me that he had paid Freeman £1,000 in cash to reserve the property at £90,000.'

He paused and looked in anguish at his wife.

'We got confused, me and Elsie.'

'So you took the law into your own hands.'

'I don't like to see Elsie upset. I confronted him at his premises and I must have pushed him too hard. He fell backwards and hit his head on the car.'

Sarah stood up and said it was time to go to the police station. As she found herself alongside Alfred Williams, she grabbed his wrist and turned it over. His knuckles were severely bruised and one finger seemed dislocated.

Alfred Williams looked Sarah in the face. 'The bastard got what he deserved.'

As they walked down the path she asked her prisoner about the disappearing estate agent's boards.

Alfred Williams laughed.

'I asked a mate of mine to nick all Freeman's boards. Problem was, he couldn't remember the firm's name so he took every one he could find. He's got enough firewood for the whole winter.'

***

Dr Hancock smiled.

'Well now, Mr Samuels, that's better: 140 over 87. I think we should keep you on the pills. I don't understand why we've not heard from the hospital. I suppose they're busy. Just one thing though. We've had the results of the blood test I took. Your liver enzyme reading, Mr Samuels... Can I suggest that you cut back to five pints a night?' she laughed.

'140 over 87?' he said. 'It's amazing what happens when your missus finds a house that you can afford.'

He left the surgery and joined his wife, who was waiting to drive him home. She decided they'd go past their new house.

***

'You're not yourself. Nick.'

He rolled over and gave his wife a cuddle. 'Tell me again what Sergeant Trimble said.'

'He said that I'm one for the future… whatever that means.'

Nick smiled with pride and gazed at his wife. 'I've had some bad news, Sarah.'

'What?'

'Our Australian PE Teacher, Imogen. She told me she's got a girlfriend back home. She said she's a lesbian.'

Sarah leaped out of bed and fetched the handcuffs. She secured her prisoner to the bed head.

'Nicholas Rudd, I'm arresting you for being sexually obsessed.'

'Have you any evidence?' he gasped.

'I'm on the case,' she chuckled.

NINE TENTHS OF THE LAW

June 2002

She lay back on the Salvador sun lounger: her husband always made certain that she had the best. She had completed her mandatory thirty lengths of their pool and made a mental note to herself, to sack the gardener on Monday. There were leaves on the bottom of the pool again. It was nearing the longest day of the year and, even before midday, the sun was already radiating its tanning rays over her body. She applied an oil-based cream to her skin and carefully placed the towel on the mattress to protect it from possible stains.

She lifted her glass of vodka and tonic and relished the cold as the mixture slid over her lips and into her mouth. She looked around her. There was no birdsong and the planes flying into Luton airport were too far away to disturb her. The combination of the solar pleasuring and the alcohol was making her feel sensual. He would be back soon. She thought she heard a nearby rustling but she looked around and felt secure in the tranquil environment.

She needed to make a decision. Her real desire was to remove both. The sensation was indescribable, heightened as it was by the knowledge that his reaction would be totally predictable.

'Top and bottom?' she asked herself.

She poured another drink. As the distillation of

water and ethanol was absorbed into her bloodstream her inhibitions dissipated. She thought she detected a scraping sound, but attributed it to one of the three cats from next door. She slowly put her hands behind her and undid the clasp of her top. It fell to her feet and she bent down to pick it up and lay it down on the table.

She relaxed into the cushion of the sun lounger and began to absorb the midday heat. Slowly she inched her hands downwards and put her thumbs into the front of her bikini bottom. She closed her eyes and pushed down. She raised herself up and completed the removal of her swimwear. She stretched forward to take it over her feet and then threw it towards the table.

She lay back and felt totally fulfilled. She sank into the softness on the cover and became seduced by the nakedness of her body: she closed her eyes and, as her dreams took over, she twitched and moved her thighs.

She had fallen half asleep when his lips kissed her fully on the mouth. She opened her eyes and radiated a smile as Emmanuel Winson beamed down at his wife.

'You are beautiful, Amoli,' he gasped.

She noticed, with some relief, that he was studying her contours.

'Perhaps some time indoors might...'

He was stopped in his tracks by the sound of crashing ladders and a cry from next door. He rushed to the nine-foot fence and pulled himself up. He gasped as he looked over at his neighbour who was picking himself up from the grass. In his hand he had a camera.

'You bastard, Alistair. You've been filming my wife.'

He climbed down and rushed into the house. In the hallway, he picked up his cricket bat and dashed outside.

Amoli was standing up and holding a towel to cover her embarrassment.

'No, Emmanuel, no violence. Not again. Please,' she shouted.

Twenty minutes later, following an emergency telephone call to the police, PC Ray Smith arrested Emmanuel Winson on suspicion of causing grievous bodily harm. He was cautioned and asked if he had anything to say. PC Rachel Simmons watched on.

'You's picking on me 'cause I'm black,' he yelled.

He was handcuffed and put into the back of the police car. He was taken to the Custody Unit at Stevenage Police Station. PC Smith explained the grounds for the arrest to the Custody Sergeant and that he had arrested the prisoner because they found him holding a cricket bat which they believed had been used to inflict serious injuries to his next door neighbour. Alistair Knight had been rushed to hospital accompanied by his wife who had made the 999 call. PC Smith showed the Custody Sergeant a camera which they had confiscated.

Sergeant Ben Higgins entered the details onto the computer system including name, date of birth, height and other personal details. He explained to Emmanuel Winson his rights, including that of having an independent solicitor free of charge.

'Fuck you, cunt. My Missus will already have called my Brief.'

'You may also,' continued Sergeant Higgins,

'consult with the Codes of Practice.'

'Bollocks.'

'I'll take it, Mr Winson, that you have no questions?' asked the Sergeant.

Emmanuel Winson spat on the floor bur remained silent.

He was searched and prepared to go into the cells.

'I'm authorising your detention at this police station, Mr Winson,' said Sergeant Higgins, noting the time

'I fucking know the Police and Criminal Evidence rules. You can't hold me for more than twenty-four hours.'

'There is an investigation that needs to be conducted, Mr Winson. You'll be treated fairly, diligently and expediently.' Sergeant Higgins paused before continuing. 'As the Custody Sergeant, I'll make sure that your welfare is paramount while you're here.'

'Fucking self-defence, you bastard,' shouted the prisoner as he was led away.

***

DC Sarah Rudd hurried into the canteen at Stevenage Police Station, ordered green tea and brown toast, and sat down. She was trying to read her notes. They were in an abbreviated form:

PEACE: plan and prepare, engage and explain, account, challenge, evaluate.

They were the five stages of a successful prisoner interview. Her eyes focused on 'challenge'. In her words, 'never believe what the bastards say.'

It was just after two o'clock and she had been on

duty since nine that morning. She must leave no later than five o'clock to collect Marcus. Her day had started much earlier with a dawn row with Nick. Their son was now two years old and Nick was objecting to picking him up from play school. Sarah had agreed to undertake the next two weeks. She was desperate to pacify him: she wanted a second child and all he could focus on was the forthcoming interview for the vacant assistant head teacher position. They needed the increase in salary that would result from a successful application.

Detective Sergeant Simon Trimble had briefed her on the arrest of Emmanuel Winson and asked her to deal with the suspect. She had made the disclosures to the solicitor, who had now arrived at the station, and who had started a private meeting with her client. She contacted DC Rudd and confirmed that they were ready to start.

Sarah called in at the Property Store and collected the key exhibit. She then trudged down to the Custody Unit where she joined Emmanuel Winson in an interview room, together with his solicitor and DC Norman Edmunson.

*P*lan and prepare.

In the short time available to her, Sarah had read the handover package, which included a summary of the arrest written by PC Ray Smith and a statement from Mrs Knight who had been seen by PC Simmonds at the hospital. She had also checked Emmanuel Winson's police file, which revealed several traffic offences and a caution following a fight in the town centre.

Sarah decided on her 'points to prove': would the accused admit to the offence of GBH? Did he accept he used a weapon (the cricket bat)? Why did he attack his neighbour? Was there an intention to harm? Was there any other provocation? She needed to gain a rapport with the assailant. She wanted an early result.

*E*ngage and explain.

'Mr Winson. This interview is being tape recorded. I am Detective Constable Sarah Rudd. Will you please introduce yourselves?' The process completed. She reminded Winson that he was entitled to free and independent legal advice. Despite the presence of his brief, the rules determined that DC Rudd had to make that statement.

'Thank you. Mr Winson, you will be entitled to ask for a copy of the tape. May I please remind you that you are under caution and so I'll repeat that for you?'

Sarah smiled and drank some water.

*A*ccount.

It was now nearing three o'clock in the afternoon and Sarah knew that she needed to complete her shift no more than two hours later so that she could collect Marcus from Play School. Her intention was to get Winson to talk. She needed to achieve agreement on what actually happened.

'Mr Winson,' she began. 'Today, Saturday, 16 June 2002, at around eleven-twenty in the morning, your next door neighbour, Alistair Fairfax Knight, sustained serious injuries. You were arrested on suspicion of causing grievous bodily harm. Can you please tell me, in your own words, what happened leading up to your arrest?'

Winson went into great detail about his perverted neighbour filming his wife over the fence and how he went round to remonstrate with him. Sarah decided it was time to change the atmosphere.

Challenge.

'Is this your possession?' Sarah asked, holding up the sporting equipment.

His solicitor whispered into his ear and he nodded at her. 'It's my cricket bat. I deny hitting anybody with it,' he said.

'Mr Winson' she said. 'Your neighbour is in hospital with severe injuries to his chest and legs. He is to have an operation later today for surgery to his spleen.' Sarah Rudd paused.

'He got what he deserved. The shit was looking over the fence and photographing my naked wife in the privacy of her garden,' sneered Winson. 'I went round to ask him not to do it again.'

'What did you say to Mr Knight?' asked DC Rudd.

'Not a lot. As soon as I reached their garden he attacked me with a golf club. I used the cricket bat to protect myself. It was self defence. He attacked me.'

Sarah looked down at her notes.

'You are around six foot three inches tall and you are aged twenty-nine years old. Mr Knight is about five-foot nine and over sixty years of age.' Sarah allowed her words to hang in the air.

'He was spying on Amoli,' said Winson. 'Have you arrested him for being a pervert?'

Emmanuel Winson lifted his glass and drank some water. His solicitor again whispered into his ear.

'You own a series of health clubs in the Home Counties, Mr Winson. If I may say so, you look as though you keep yourself in good shape. Did you know that Mr. Knight had a minor stroke last year?' continued Sarah.

'Well, it didn't stop him taking pictures of Amoli. She was naked.'

'Please tell me what happened, Mr Winson.'

He looked at his legal adviser and she nodded. 'Amoli was sunbathing in our back garden. She now recalls that on several occasions she thought that she heard a sound. I got home and as I was greeting her, there was a crashing sound from next door. I looked over the fence and Alistair was lying on the grass, holding a camera. I went round to remonstrate with him. My Amoli has a beautiful body and I'm the only person who sees it.'

DC Rudd was already satisfied that she could break down the story being told by the accused. She glanced at the solicitor, who she sensed had already conceded the case.

'Mr Winson. Can we just recap on what took place when you went round to remonstrate with your next door neighbour?'

Winson was beginning to become restless. 'His wife was helping him get up. She hates us blacks. She hates the fact I'm richer than him. They told us he has a civil service pension and it's not enough for them to live on.'

'So you are friends with Mr. Knight? You must be if he talks about his private finances,' said DC Rudd.

'They patronise us. I went to Cambridge: the university. I got brains. My father made money in hotels in Antigua.'

'So what happened when you confronted Mr Knight?'

'He had a golf club in his hand. His wife was shouting at him. He lunged at me and I used the bat to deflect his weapon.'

DC Rudd looked down at her notes.

'Did you not say, Mr Winson, that when you

reached their garden, Mrs Knight was helping her husband get up after he fell off the ladders? Was he not holding the camera in his hand?'

'There was shouting. He must 'ave got up. He attacked me with a golf club.'

'Where did he get that from, Mr Winson?'

'Fuck knows. He was waving it at me.'

DC Rudd again looked down at her notes. 'Was he holding it in his hand when you looked over the fence?' she asked.

'It was on the fucking ground. He'd fallen off the ladders and hurt himself. That's what warned us the fucking pervert was filming my Amoli.'

'Was it on his left or his right side?'

'What's that about? He fucking attacked me.'

DC Rudd paused. She thought it was time to break down his defence. 'Can you show me your injuries please, Mr Winson?'

'What fucking injuries? The bastard missed me.'

His solicitor whispered urgently in his ear.

'So how did Mr Knight sustain his injuries, Mr. Winson?'

'Dunno. He fell over.'

Now the real 'challenge' came quickly from the police officer. Over the next few minutes, she repeatedly proved that he was lying.

'Did you use the cricket bat to attack him?' she asked.

'He attacked me with the golf club.'

'Mr Winson. Why did you stop in the hallway of your home to collect the cricket bat before confronting Mr Knight?' asked DC Rudd.

'To defend myself.'

She paused and then spoke in a firm voice. 'But,

Mr Winson, you have said that when you looked over the fence you had seen that Mr Knight was hurt. Why did you need a cricket bat to defend yourself against an injured man?'

'He fucking attacked me!'

'Did he hurt you?'

His solicitor tried to halt the interview but the accused exploded.

'Fuck the lot of you. He got what the pervert deserved!' he shouted. He looked at the cricket bat. 'I wish I'd hit him a fucking load more.'

*E*valuate.

His solicitor folded her arms and sighed. DC Rudd summarised her conclusions.

'Before I turn off the tape, is there anything else you want to say, Mr.Winson?'

'You're coming on me 'cause I'm black. No court will convict me. So go and fuck yourself, DC Rudd.'

Sarah switched off the tape. She told the prisoner that she was going to leave him with his solicitor. She went to see the Custody Sergeant, went through the evidence with him and asked that Winson be charged and remanded in custody.

'If he gets bail, there must be conditions. He's dangerous, Sarge.'

***

At around four-fifty in the afternoon Sarah briefed DS Trimble.

'Good, well done DC Rudd, and don't forget to write up your notes this afternoon and get that property booked back in.'

She picked up the cricket bat and left his office.

Her mobile phone rang and she listened as Nick reminded her that she had to pick up Marcus. She looked at her watch: she had seven minutes remaining before the due time. As she looked at the cricket bat in her hands, her friend PC Rachel Grainger shouted a greeting.

'Rachel,' responded Sarah. 'Be a mate and book this back into the Property Store for me, will you? I've got to collect Marcus.'

'It'll cost you, Sarah. All the gossip you've heard.'

She laughed and agreed to meet the following day. She collected Marcus and that evening she drank some wine as Nick thrilled her with the news of his impending promotion.

***

The trial of Emanuel Clive Winson took place some weeks later at Stevenage Magistrates Court. Sarah had been told to be available from ten o'clock. She had intended to travel over with the arresting officer PC Ray Smith. At ten minutes past nine, Sarah visited the Property Store only to discover that the cricket bat was missing. She then ascertained that PC Rachel Grainger was on leave. She managed to speak to her at her Devon holiday cottage. She could not remember what she had done with it. She agreed to speak to the Duty Sergeant and gave permission for her locker to be searched. The weapon was missing.

She spoke to DS Trimble, who exploded.

'You've got two options, DC Rudd. You can tell the Prosecutor and he can try to do a deal with the Defence or you can try to bluff your way through.

At around eleven-thirty later that morning, the

Defence Lawyer discovered that the weapon with which his client was accused of using in the assault of Alistair Knight, was not available.

'It's in the Police Station,' stuttered Sarah when questioned.

The private views of the Prosecutor were still ringing in her ears.

'Are you suggesting, DC Rudd, that the Magistrates hold up this trial while you go back to the Police Station and collect it?'

'Does it matter?' asked Sarah.

The Prosecutor groaned and put his hands to his head.

'May I please ask, DC Rudd, does what matter?'

'I've interviewed the accused. He's not arguing that he went round to Mr Knight's house with the cricket bat.'

'Perhaps he was playing cricket for his local team, DC Rudd?' suggested the lawyer.

'He was intent on beating the living daylights out of Mr Knight.'

'You were there, were you, DC Rudd?'

'Of course not. You know that. I interviewed Mr Winson. He argued it was self defence. We all know that's rubbish.'

The defence lawyer smiled. A case he had expected to lose was about to be turned into a victory.

'DC Rudd, where is the cricket bat?'

'It's somewhere in Stevenage Police Station,' she said.

'Somewhere? Surely it's in the Property Store correctly marked up as an exhibit, DC Rudd.'

'I wish it was,' spluttered Sarah.

The Magistrate intervened and asked both

solicitors to approach the bench. Sarah looked up to see Emmanuel Winson grinning from ear to ear.

***

'If I may say so, Sarge, you're taking this rather calmly.'

DS Simon Trimble smiled.

'You're not going to forget this one in a hurry are you, Sarah?' he asked.

'It was horrible. I was humiliated.'

'No, you made a fool of the Force. Never again Sarah, understood?'

'But a vicious thug is free because of the system. Everyone in the Court knew he was guilty.'

'Sarah. Possession is nine tenth of the law and you did not have the assault weapon. You messed up badly. Got it? Let's move on.'

DS Trimble smiled and picked up a file off his desk.

'We're raiding three of Emmanuel Winson's health clubs tomorrow morning. He's running a VAT fraud on gym equipment. He buys it on the continent, claims the VAT back which he's never paid in the first place, and then supplies it for cash to other clubs.'

Detective Sergeant Simon Trimble laughed. 'The scales of justice work in a funny way.'

Sarah moved towards the door. 'Thank you, Sarge.'

'Never again, Sarah. Agreed?'

DC Sarah Rudd turned back and looked at her boss. 'Never again, Sarge. That's a promise.'

She left DS Trimble's office and breathed a sigh of

utter relief.

***

Sarah arrived home to find that Marcus, after an afternoon at the park, had been bathed and was sound asleep in his bed. She checked the monitoring system and relaxed. Nick appeared, wearing light grey slacks and a plain white shirt. Sarah's breath caught in her throat at the sight of her handsome husband.

'Have you had a good day, darling?' he asked.

'I arrested seventeen shoplifters, three murderers and found Lord Lucan,' she said.

'Well done, Sarah. That's impressive.'

He led her into the dining room, where the curtains were partly closed. There was a candle burning in the centre of the table which had been laid out for two people. He picked up a glass of champagne and handed it to her. He reached for a second and touched her glass. She noticed that the bottle was half empty.

'To us,' he proposed. 'I'm just finishing off the main course. Go and change: I'll be ready for you when you come downstairs.'

Sarah reached the shower and stood naked underneath its powerful waters. She then dried herself, dressed and returned back to the dining room. They began with a supermarket starter comprising special offer crab meat, coleslaw, potato salad and chopped tomatoes. Nick had selected a Chardonnay and poured them each a generous glass.

'Would you like the good news, the good news or the good news?' he asked.

'The Australia PE teacher is not a lesbian and is

having an affair with you, you're planning to leave home so I can find a decent lover and we've won the Lottery.'

Nick thought briefly about Imogen, the Aussie temptress. He swallowed but quickly regained his poise.

'Close. I've won the position for the Assistant Head Teacher. Out of ten candidates. Little me, Sarah.'

She leaped up from her chair and ran to him. She threw her arms around his head and promised him unlimited sex for the next ten years. She sat down and drank some wine.

'Is there more good news?'

'My Dad. He's clear. It's non-malignant.'

During the last few weeks, Reginald Rudd had been undergoing tests for suspected cancer of the prostate. It was the news they had wanted but thought might not been possible.

'He's having an operation in two days time but that is to remove the growth.'

'We must be there, Nick. Your Mum will need us.'

'Yes. Thanks. Much to do.'

'Is there a third lot of good news?' asked Sarah.

'I've solved our financial problems, Sarah.'

'No, Nick! We've been through this. We're not selling our house.'

'Agreed. We're not selling this place.'

He stood up and went round to sit by her.

'Sarah. It's all the talk in the staff room. There's this mortgage lender, the Northern Rock Building Society. I've been to see them. They asked me how much did I want. I've filled in the forms. It's called 'self certification': you are on trust to tell the truth.

They approved our application in two days.'

'Our application, Nick. I've not applied for anything.'

'We're having an extra twenty thousand pounds and the rate of interest is fixed for five years. Even with the increased amount the payment per month is lower than we've been paying.'

'Assuming interest levels don't go up, Nick.'

'Sarah. You've heard what Gordon Brown, The Chancellor of the Exchequer, is saying. He's ended boom and bust. The economy is going to prosper for the next ten years and Nick and Sarah Rudd are going with it. I've brought some holiday brochures for you to read.'

Sarah looked across at her husband, who had returned to his chair.

'There's something I'd rather have, Nick,' she said as she undid the buttons on her dress. As they went upstairs, the roast loin of pork in the oven began to turn rather crispy.

***

At around two-thirty in the early hours of the next morning Nick went downstairs to find Sarah in the dining room with papers laid out over the table. She was reading the agreement from the Building Society.

'You need to sign just the one form, Sarah,' he said.

'We'll owe what this house is worth, Nick. If we try to settle early there are huge redemption charges. It reverts to normal rates after five years. So what happens if Mr Brown is wrong?'

'Just think of the life we can give Marcus and

number two, Sarah.'

'Yes, let's live dangerously,' she said. 'One point, Nick. It says here that if we fail to keep up the repayments, the house reverts back to Northern Rock.'

'They always say that, Sarah. It's our house. We live here. And remember something else.'

'What, Nick?'

'Possession is nine tenths of the law.'

I'M PARTIAL TO A DRINK OR THREE

November 2002

It was the fifth of November and Sarah was regretting her decision to agree to Nick taking their son to the neighbour's bonfire party. She had extracted promises and guarantees that Marcus would be under the control of his father at all times and would not be allowed within thirty yards of the flames. She knew she was being overly protective, but she was his mother.

Her concerns were not helped by the insistence of Dr Christina Howe to lecture the assembled group of seventeen police officers on the dangers of alcoholism. They were there at the command of the Chief Constable of Hertfordshire, who had a theory that crime could be reduced if his officers understood better the effects of the excessive consumption of alcohol.

The local Health Centre was busy but they were hidden away in a back room. Sarah groaned as the session continued.

'I qualified at Bart's in 1999,' informed Dr Howe, 'and spent two years as a Registrar at a GP Training Practice in North London before becoming a partner here.' She paused. 'My task today is to explain the problems of drink.' She looked around her. 'Many of us believe that alcoholism is best understood if defined as an individual who cannot go two days without a drink.'

There was a collective intake of breath as a majority wondered if they should sign up for 'Alcoholics Anonymous' there and then.

'We doctors disagree amongst ourselves. Some will argue it is the uncontrolled consumption of alcoholic beverages whilst others think that is simply excessive drinking. I had a woman in my surgery only yesterday who is a member of 'it's twelve noon, time for my glass of sherry' brigade. When we calculated her weekly unit intake, it was around twenty- two and, as she would almost certainly be lying to me, we can assume it is possibly nearer thirty, which is far too high.'

A hand went up. PC Charlie Hill asked if he could ask a question. Dr Howe nodded.

'When, at eleven-thirty on a Friday night, a yobbo punches me in my balls and then pukes all over me, is he an alcoholic?'

'He's under arrest,' laughed PC Georgina Cummings.

'It's a serious question,' retorted PC Hill.

'And a good question,' continued Dr Howe. 'A drunk is not necessarily an alcoholic.'

'Well, let me assure you, Doctor, that the yobbo has no intention of going two days without a drink. As soon as we release him, he'll be off to the boozer.'

'Well, it's only one of the measures we doctors use. As I say, we ask our patients about their weekly consumption. Anything over twenty-two units causes us a worry.'

'So if a patient admits to drinking, say more than twenty-five units a week, you are saying he or she is an alcoholic?' asked DC Pamela Green.

'No, I'm not saying that. It's simply a sign to us that there is excessive consumption,' said Dr Howe.

'What do you do about it?' asked DC Green.

'Well I'm a very busy doctor. In a ten minute surgery appointment all I can do...'

'You do fuck all. You let the patient out and expect us to clear up the mess,' said PC Hill.

'No, no. The Chief Constable's idea is that we should work together on these issues.'

'You've just admitted the truth: there's nothing you can do,' said Pamela Green.

A hand was placed on Dr Howe's shoulder and she sat down. Dr Gerald Taylor, who was the senior partner at the Practice, looked at the police officers.

'We are lost in admiration for the work you do. Dr Howe is one of the brilliant young doctors who are being trained in modern medical methods. We want to work with the other agencies. I can assure you that ten years ago the only way you'd get in here would be by making an appointment!'

There was a ripple of laugher.

'What we are talking about is alcoholism. That is not excessive drinking. That is to be regretted and I sympathise with the young officer who had his testicles kicked.'

'Most exciting thing that's happened to him in years,' laughed Georgina Cummings.

Dr Taylor smiled.

'There is a point I need to make here. The Friday night yobbo, to use your term for him, PC Hill.'

'Charlie has a way with words,' chuckled PC Cummings.

'He's almost certainly a binge drinker. He'll have worked hard during the week and on Friday night, he lets off steam. I'm not trying to excuse him but medically, the amount these kids drink is simply too much for their system.'

Dr. Taylor looked around the room. His own daughter was causing him and his wife enormous problems with her excessive use of alcohol, soft drugs and now they had become aware of secret funding from loan arrangers. He sighed deeply.

'This is not going to impress you but we ourselves don't really know the difference between heavy drinking, excessive drinking and alcoholism. All of them damage the patient's health but there again there are usually other factors at work. What the Chief Constable has recognised is that if we can help you understand the subject better, you may be able to deal with the incidences you attend more effectively.'

'So tell us, Doctor. What should we look for?'

'Your name please?'

'Detective Constable Sarah Rudd.'

'Well, DC Rudd, you've asked the key question. How do we spot an alcoholic?'

'They fall over,' laughed DC Green.

Sarah looked daggers at her. She was now interested in the discussion.

'Right DC Rudd, I'll give you five clear signs:

'One: an alcoholic loses all sense of time. The lady who Dr Howe mentioned, the twelve o'clock sherry drinker, she's lonely. Drink is her companion. She's not an alcoholic.

'Two: they lie to themselves. Many alcoholics convince themselves they are moderate drinkers.

'Three: they often choose to drink only vodka; it's odourless and many alcoholics spend their lives with vodka inside them.

'Four: and this, DC Rudd, is our real difficulty. They are compellingly convincing. I'm a good doctor, I promise you. I had a woman patient, a mother with three children, and for two years I missed the fact she was drinking herself to death. In fact, she did just that. I will tell you, I still think about her. I let her down.'

'She let herself and her children down,' said DC Green.

Dr Taylor sighed.

'Her partner was into anal sex. He made her have relationships every night. Sometimes it was worse than that. She was drinking to try to keep going for the sake of her children. In the end, he infected her and she came to me too late.'

DC Rudd punctured the silence that followed. 'You said there are five signs, Dr Taylor?' she asked.

'They hide drink, DC Rudd.' He paused. 'The alcoholic is one of the most cunning people you'll ever meet. Their partners often don't know. They'll bury containers in the garden so they can sneak out at night for a drink. Where there is a lock and a key there may be hidden bottles.' He paused. 'Never fall for the obvious. I did and I lost a patient.'

Dr Taylor paused.

'It may sound daft but there is another sign. They use mouthwash. They will carry round little flasks full of the stuff with them.'

***

It was taking time for Sarah and Nick Rudd to rebuild their lives after the conclusion of the events surrounding the Australian PE teacher, Imogen. Nick recognised that Sarah had been hurt by his brief disloyalty and he was treading carefully. Their situation was not helped by the fact that when she arrived at the fireworks party, Marcus was nowhere to be seen. He was found eight minutes later upstairs in a bedroom watching a *'Thomas the Tank Engine'* DVD. Nick had become distracted by a French-speaking guest who wanted to try out her vocabulary on him.

As they later walked back to their home, he asked her about her day.

'It was spoilt by being reminded that next week is my turn as the Night Detective.' Sarah paused. 'Same old shit,' she mused.

***

The following week, Sarah was pleased to find herself on the same shift as her friend, Rachel Grainger. They were similar in looks and temperament, but there the similarities ended. Rachel loved being a PC, but for her it was a job. She played by the clock and by the book. They drank coffee in the canteen and agreed that their favourite song for the year was by Nickelback.

'How you remind me,' sang Sarah.

'This time I'm mistaken. For handing you a heart worth breaking,' sang Rachel and together they reprised, *'Yeah, yeah, yeah, no, no.'*

It was around one-thirty in the morning when a call came in to the Control Room. An ambulance driver was reporting from the scene of a domestic dispute that there were children present and the police should attend. This was happening anyway and, as a Domestic Incident always requires two officers,

Rachel persuaded Sarah to go with her: they quickly reached their car and arrived at Culver Close in a little over eight minutes.

The medic was on the doorstep waiting for them.

'She says she made a mistake. She's refusing treatment although she's holding her stomach. He's not said a word.'

'Who made the call?' asked Rachel.

'Her name is Norma Dutton. She did. We're off.'

The two police officers went down the hall and into the kitchen. There were two people sitting at the table. Sarah went to separate the couple, but found herself overtaken by PC Grainger who sat down with them and started talking.

Norma Dutton nodded her head and the man said nothing. Sarah quickly ran up the steps and through the door with Winnie the Pooh on the outside. There were two small infants in separate cots: there was a monitor, which she checked and which was in working order. The room was immaculately tidy. Sarah returned to the kitchen.

'This is my colleague, DC Rudd,' said PC Grainger. 'Sarah. This is Norma Dutton and her partner, Keith Patton.'

'Why did you phone 999?' asked Sarah.

'I've established that, DC Rudd. Norma was gripped with stomach pains. She phoned the emergency services but now feels better.'

'You're a mother,' said Sarah. 'Just the two children?'

'Yes. Twins. Boy and girl.'

'So how do you feel about this, Mr Patton?' asked Sarah.

'You can go away, thank you. It was good of you

to come but we do not need the police.'

'I'd be happier if you'd let the hospital check you over, Norma,' said Sarah.

'I'm fine, thank you.' She then looked at Rachel and smiled.

'Do you mind if I look around?' asked Sarah.

'Why?' Mr Patton clenched his fists. He seemed older and had grey flecks of hair. 'Stay here. I need the loo.'

He returned a few minutes later and Sarah smelt it.

'You can go where you like,' he said.

She completed a thorough check of the whole house. It was clean and well managed. The garden was mainly laid to lawn with a shed at the bottom. The door was locked.

As PC Grainger and DC Rudd drove back to the station, Sarah asked if she had smelt it.

'Smelt what?' she asked as she parked the car.

'Mouthwash. When he came back from the toilet. He'd used it.'

Rachel parked the car in the Station secure area and slammed the door.

'I think Detective Rudd is getting carried away. Were the children secure?'

'They were fine, Rachel. It was her. Norma. She wasn't.'

'If she says she's happy not to seek medical attention and the children are safe, what more can we do?'

'So why did you not separate them, Rachel?' Sarah hesitated. 'It's standard procedure, you should know that.'

Rachel sneered. 'You'd see a crime in every showing of 'Tom and Jerry" she shouted.

'So why did she dial 999?' asked Sarah.

***

Two nights later, Sarah and Rachel were friends again and were discussing their choice of films for the weekend.

'Nick wants to see *Harry Potter and the Chamber of Secrets*. He says he must understand what his pupils are watching but I don't believe that,' said Sarah. 'I understand that Harry is plagued by a strange voice. It will be like my mother-in-law visiting us!'

They laughed together and put their hands around the warm coffee cups. Rachel was back after having been called out to an incident at the local refuge centre, where two tramps had decided to set fire to their mattresses in protest at their lack of supper.

'Well, I'm off to see *Spider-Man*. I do wonder if my Liam is genetically modified,' laughed Rachel.

The call came in, again from the emergency services, and Sarah attached herself to Rachel as she set out for Culver Road. This time, as they entered the home, she went straight upstairs but, again, the twins were sound asleep and being monitored correctly.

When she reached the kitchen, Norma Dutton was making a pot of tea. Rachel was sitting at the table looking out of the window. There was frost on the glass. Sarah flared. PC Grainer had again failed to separate the couple.

'So sorry, Officer,' said Keith Patton. 'You can go now.'

'Norma, are you ok?' asked Sarah.

'I'm fine.'

'No stomach pains?' she asked.

Norma Dutton looked at her. 'I'm fine.'

'So who phoned 999?' asked Sarah.

'I thought that Keith was having a turn,' she replied.

'A turn,' repeated Sarah. 'How are you feeling, Mr Patton?'

'Sorry. I need the toilet.'

He came back some minutes later and Sarah edged up close to him.

'Damn,' she said. 'I forgot to get Nick his beers. Is there an all-night off-licence near here?' she asked.

'You're asking the wrong people,' said Mr Patton. 'Norma and me don't drink.'

'Not at all?' exclaimed PC Grainger.

'Norma likes a sherry but I stopped three years ago.'

'Why?' asked Sarah.

'I took up golf. My knees are too weak for squash. I decided to get fit. I'm down to a handicap of fourteen. Not bad, eh?'

'You must have played squash into your forties, Mr Patton?'

'I stopped at fifty-two years of age.'

'And you never touch alcohol?'

'Not good for you, Officer. It's a killer. My health and my responsibilities for my children are too great to ruin my life with drink.'

As they returned back to the police station, they had a serious disagreement.

'You're letting your ambition overtake you, Sarah,' said Rachel. 'It was innocent. We all make mistakes.'

'Did you smell the mouthwash? What did Dr Taylor tell us?'

'Give me one piece of evidence that requires us to investigate any further,' said Rachel.

'Two calls for an ambulance,' said Sarah. 'And while we're at it, this has to be referred to Social Services: have you checked the records?'

'Happens all the time. The medic told me he was called out for a toothache earlier in the evening.' She paused. 'It's something and nothing, Sarah.'

Rachel stopped and turned towards Sarah. 'Were the children sleeping soundly and was there a monitor?'

'Yes,' said Sarah.

'Did Norma Dutton look as though she needed any help?'

'No,' said Sarah.

'Did Keith Patton give a totally rational explanation to your questions about alcohol?'

Sarah nodded her head.

'So give me one bit of evidence that required us to do any more. And don't mention fucking mouthwash.'

'Did you see any golf equipment in the house?' asked Sarah.

***

When the call came through the following evening, PC Rachel Grainger told Sarah that she'd rather go to Culver Road with another officer.

'They're all out,' said Sarah, 'and I'm coming.'

When they reached the house, the ambulance driver was quite apologetic.

'Sorry. False alarm. The woman fell over in the kitchen. She bruised her head and I'd prefer she go to hospital but she is saying she's fine.'

'So why did you contact us?' asked Sarah.

'Dunno. Instinct, I suppose. Cheerio.'

Rachel had insisted on checking the children and so Sarah left Norma in the kitchen and asked Mr Patton to join her in the lounge.

'I'm so sorry, Officer' said Keith Patton as he sat down. 'Poor Norma slipped on a wet patch and I felt she might need medical attention.'

'At two in the morning?' asked Sarah.

'What difference does that make? We always watch our children.' He stood up. 'I'll be back.'

'The kids are fine,' said Rachel and then went into the kitchen. 'How are you, Norma?'

She did not reply.

Keith Patton came back in.

'Excuse me saying so Mr Patton, but I love the smell of your mouthwash.'

'Thanks,' he said. He picked up several pieces of paper. 'Want to see my dental bills. I've got an infected wisdom tooth. I have to wash my mouth out every four hours. The antibiotics are taking ages to work.'

Rachel looked daggers at her companion.

'Perhaps a large scotch might help,' suggested Sarah.

'If I drank, it probably would,' he replied.

'I'd love to see your golf equipment, Mr Patton,' said Sarah.

PC Grainger stood up and grabbed Sarah by the collar.

'We're off. Glad you're feeling better, Norma. Phone us if you need us.'

She dragged DC Rudd outside, whereupon Sarah

knew something was wrong. She allowed herself to be pulled back to the car.

'I'm fucking fed up with you, Sarah. Think of yourself as Inspector Morse. It was nothing. Get in and shut up.'

'You go, Rachel. I'm going to walk back,' said Sarah.

She slowly trod carefully on the icy pavement and tried to grasp what she had seen. She went over and over the facts. The three 999 calls, the look Norma gave her, the authority exuded by Keith Patton, his word-perfect rejection of alcohol, the immaculate house, the children safely asleep and being carefully monitored, the locked shed and the mouthwash. She re-read the dental bills: they were real.

She stumbled as she ran into a dustbin not returned back from the morning collection.

'What had Dr Taylor said? What were the five signs?'

She sat down and put her hands to her head.

And then she knew. They had missed the obvious.

She ran back as fast as possible and she checked. The boot of the car was damaged and half open. She lifted it up. There were empty bottles of vodka. She ran to the front door and rang the bell. There were no lights and there was no reply. But she thought that she heard a moaning sound. She reached for her radio.

'This is DC Rudd. I'm at 26 Culver Road. I'm going in. I need back-up and medical support.'

She picked up a large stone from the porch and smashed the front door glass. She put her hand through and found the handle. She threw open the door and rushed down the hall into the kitchen. She found the light switch. Norma Dutton was lying on the floor in a pool of blood. In the corner, a man was being violently sick. She ran upstairs and found the children: they were sound asleep.

As she returned to the kitchen, she heard the sirens. She looked at the man and went to the aid of the woman.

'I'm pregnant,' she gasped. 'He didn't want it.'

Sarah found herself being lifted out of the way as the medics rushed to attend to Norma. A doctor was already leaning over Keith Patton.

'Drunk as a Lord,' he said.

'But I was here less than an hour ago. He was as sober as a judge,' pleaded Sarah.

'There's nobody more deceitful than an alcoholic,' said the doctor.

As Norma was stretchered out of the house to the ambulance, Sarah walked beside her.

'I could have helped you, Norma,' she pleaded.

'It's beyond that now,' she gasped.

'The law can protect you from men like him,' she said.

Norma looked up. 'He's my brother,' she said.

'You'd hidden his drink in your car?'

'Yes. But he always finds it,' she gasped.

***

Nick had waited up and was standing in front of her as she slumped back into their lounge sofa. She was clenching a glass of gin and had not bothered to add any tonic water. He was holding out his right hand and shaking it.

'Do you drink and drive? No, I spill most of it.'

128

He roared with laughter.

'There's a whole series of alcohol jokes doing the rounds at school,' he explained. 'He's a legend in his own lunchtime,' he chuckled.

Sarah continued to stare at him.

'You'll like this one, darling,' he said. 'Beauty is in the eye of the beer holder.'

Her face remained impassive.

'It's a play on words. Beer holder... beholder... have you lost your sense of humour?'

She took a deep drink and allowed the alcohol to linger in her mouth.

He now added to his performance by adopting a silly face.

'Should a midget drink in a mini-bar?' he roared.

Sarah continued to gaze at the floor.

'This is a good one, Sarah.' He combined his silly face with a hunched-up posture. 'I'm partial to a drink or three,' he slurred.

'Nick,' said Sarah.

'Yes, darling'

'Fuck off.'

THE SUPPER GROUP

January 2003

Seventy-two hours after Gavin and Sheelagh Eastman hosted their supper group, several lives of the people who attended would change forever.

***

'So I'm the little wife at home, am I?' shouted Sarah Rudd.

'Don't be ridiculous,' answered her husband. 'Gavin Eastman came round an hour ago. You were, as usual, late home. He said that he and his wife are holding what he calls their 'supper group' on Friday and would we like to attend? I said 'yes'.'

'Without asking me. What about Marcus?'

'Their daughter, Lauren, is babysitting for us.'

'Oh. We can afford staff now, can we? I'm not having a stranger looking after my son.'

'They live two doors away and it's about time we had a life. Lauren is fourteen.'

Sarah threw her coat towards the hall cupboard door. 'I think we're 'rent-a-crowd'. To ask us with two days to go. They're short of people.'

Nick lifted his glass of lager to his lips and drank deeply. He looked at his angered wife. The tiffs were getting more regular. His problems with Imogen and her attack on Sarah were too recent to dismiss. Nick

131

had thought that the chance of getting out together might help them.

'Gavin was upfront on that. It's a regular monthly event and they take it in turns to host the occasion. One of the couples has dropped out because of family illness.'

'We don't know these people, Nick.'

'Then I suggest we make an effort to integrate.'

'It's not that easy,' sighed Sarah.

Over the next forty-eight hours, her mood did not improve. Eventually, the time reached seven-thirty on Friday evening and Sheelagh Eastman arrived with Lauren. Somewhat to Sarah's surprise, she inspected the house so that her daughter was familiar with all the rooms and the exits. She examined the alarm system and watched Marcus sleeping peacefully. She gave instructions that Lauren would not watch television: she would be concentrating on her studies. She checked the phone line and made a test call to Gavin. She concluded by telling her daughter that either she or her father would come round every hour to check-up on her.

'We'll see you soon,' said Sheelagh Eastman as she kissed a smiling Lauren.

Sarah went upstairs and changed her dress. She put on a black outfit over a green blouse and took off her tights. She added some jewellery and increased her use of perfume. She found Nick waiting for her in the hallway. He nodded his approval and felt a surge of adrenalin. They strolled together through the cold evening air and found the door to the Eastman's house opening as they arrived. Almost immediately, they were ushered into the lounge and given glasses of wine. The atmosphere was electric. The background music was from the London shows. The lighting was limited to surrounding wall illuminations. It was subtle and atmospheric.

'Eat and drink,' instructed Gavin Eastman, pointing to the buffet table.

Despite the absence of any introductions, Sarah found herself striking up a friendship with Roman Gainsborough. His opening chat-up line was unusual.

'That's Ollie over there. He's my partner. So, darling, you're safe with me but watch out for him,' he warned pointing to a tall greyish-going-white haired man. 'Says he's a doctor but I'm not sure. He's not examining my private parts, I tell you. Now, what's your name? You're gorgeous. You could put me off Ollie,' he roared.

At that moment, the lights went on and Gavin Eastman invited everybody to take a seat. Sarah found herself with Ollie on one side and a woman on the other.

'Good evening Supper Group members and invited guests.'

Everyone burst into applause and hugged somebody. Sarah noticed that the wine bottles were now being passed around and hot food was being served by a waitress, whose outfit would not have disgraced a Bunny Club. Sarah tried the fried prawns, which she dipped into the barbeque sauce. She then sampled the fish and chips in a cornet and followed this up with a mini-beef burger bap.

'Roll-call first,' continued Gavin. 'Nancy and Gilbert are in Cornwall with her rather poorly mother, so I'm delighted to introduce to you Nick and Sarah Rudd, our neighbours. Nick teaches French and is Assistant Head Teacher at our local school and

Sarah is a police officer.'

There was a huge cheer and a round of applause.

'Tell me, darling,' shouted Roman in Sarah's direction. 'Have you brought your truncheon?' The laughter took time to subside. Sarah fixed a stare, stood up and went over to him where she put her head towards his and spoke in a loud voice.

'I have got my truncheon with me, Roman, and I'm going to tell you exactly where I'm going to put it.' She muzzled her mouth over his ear.

'Oh. Lionel Blair. All my Christmas's have come at once,' he exclaimed.

'That's the introduction to Roman and Ollie completed,' chuckled Gavin. 'Nick, they are my financial advisers and they are wonderful people.'

'Only because you are building a marvellous business, Gavin,' said Ollie. He turned to Sarah. 'Gavin and Sheelagh are from County Antrim. They stopped farming and came over here with not much money and an idea. What 'Tractor-stop' does is make the braking systems for tractors. They supply nearly all the main manufacturers.'

'Ollie,' interrupted Roman. 'Tell Nick and Sarah what's so clever about their company.' They looked at Gavin, who nodded his agreement.

'Well,' continued Ollie. 'What Gavin does is to pay for the development of the braking system from his own resources so that if, and when, the tractors are made commercially they have the contract to supply the part. He is building up a wonderful business.'

'Nearly went bust, Ollie,' said Gavin. 'You and Roman saved the day getting me that foreign loan.'

'Sheelagh,' said Nick. 'Sheelagh,' he repeated. 'It is a beautiful name.'

The hostess blushed. 'I'm just an Irish girl, Nick.'

'It's from the Latin word '*Caelia*' meaning 'heavenly',' he said. Her eyes went to the ceiling as she melted at his charm.

Gavin looked at the two supper group members sitting either side of Nick.

'Dr Alan and Dr Lucinda Brown,' he announced. 'They are doctors,' he continued.

The laughter filled the room again. She spoke up.

'We're partners in a City Centre practice,' she said. 'We have two adopted children, Ben and Rosie.'

'From Zimbabwe,' said Sheelagh.

'We don't talk about that,' said Lucinda. 'They needed a home. We have given them one.'

Sarah felt herself going cold. She was searching for a file in her mind.

'Drinks done, all lights on, music off,' instructed Gavin. 'Nick, Sarah, we have a tradition with our supper group. We have to discuss one serious matter before the party starts.'

'Gracious,' thought Sarah. 'I thought it had begun.'

'Right. Tonight's question comes from Sheelagh Eastman of no fixed abode. 'Does the group think that Hans Blix will find weapons of mass destruction in Iraq?"

'Without a doubt,' responded Nick. 'The UN Chief Weapons Inspector would not be in Baghdad unless he had reliable information. Tony Blair is handling things perfectly. He and George Bush, since 9/11, have made the world a safer place. By taking out Saddam Hussein, which I am certain is what will be attempted, we will remove the worst tyrant we have seen for many years.'

'You haven't met Robert Mugabe,' said Alan

Brown.

Over the next fifteen minutes, the discussion ranged far and wide. Sarah was diverted from her growing admiration for her articulate husband by a mental search for some Intelligence they had received.

Gavin Eastman rang a bell.

'Time's up Supper Group members,' he suggested. 'Now for more wine and food.' The lights were dimmed.

Nick turned to Lucinda Brown, who had her hand on his knee.

'Did you go to Zimbabwe to find your children?' he asked.

'We don't talk about it,' she replied. 'What is more interesting is your job. Assistant Head. You're doing rather well.'

Sarah removed Ollie's hand from her thigh and looked across at her husband, who was now committed to an animated conversation with his fellow guest.

Ten minutes later, the lights went on and Gavin called for quiet.

'It's music time,' he announced. 'Nick, Sarah. We have a second tradition. The Group has bought a karaoke machine which is here.' He pointed to the equipment being moved from behind the sofa. 'We three couples have each put a musical suggestion in an envelope so I have six offerings. Can be anything/anyone: solo, group, a song from a show, Cliff Richard.' There were groans of disapproval. 'Sarah, I'm going to ask you to choose one.' He walked over and she selected a package from the end. He opened it and started to read the wording on the paper.

'This is from Dr Alan Brown.' There was polite applause. 'Alan says that the three girls must dress accordingly and perform '*Sound of the Underground*' by Girls Aloud.' He took a tape out of the envelope and put it in the machine. There was a roar of approval.

Sarah was in turmoil. This was not her scene and she was still searching for a half-remembered fact. She looked at Nick in despair. But Sheelagh was already in control of rehearsals.

'Girls. Upstairs,' she instructed. 'Gavin. Get the room ready and boys, prepare yourselves for a female fantasia.'

She found herself swept along by events. Nick had not missed an episode of '*Popstars: The Rivals*' the previous autumn and Sarah had been prevented by her duties from seeing them on only two occasions. Nick simply ogled at the gyrations of the five singers and Sarah sensed that Kimberley Walsh was his favourite. Even she wondered how he could not choose the allure of Cheryl Cole although, for her, Sarah Harding was stunning.

They had reached an unoccupied front room, which was clearly used by Gavin and Sheelagh as a changing area. For no reason at all, Sarah worked out that their two daughters must share. *Lucky Louis*, she thought. *A bedroom to himself.*

Sheelagh was handing out the words of the Girls Aloud hit song '*Sound of the Underground*'.

Sarah hesitated. 'How did you know that it would this song?' she spluttered.

'Now, now, Sarah. You're off duty tonight,' chided Sheelagh. 'All the envelopes contained the same choice. My Gavin fiddled it. She roared with laughter. 'He'll do anything to see me wearing very little.'

Well. He can forget that, thought Sarah and then she realised that Sheelagh and Lucinda were undressing.

'Lots of breasts and thighs are called for,' said Sheelagh. 'And bare feet.'

She had now produced some short skirts and thin, white blouses. Sarah noticed that her own change of outfit was carefully chosen for the fuller figure. Lucinda was without a surplus ounce of flesh but Sarah knew she still had, at the age of thirty-two, a sensual body provided she restricted the intake of canteen breakfasts.

This was not for her, but did she have a choice? Marcus was safe, the drink was flowing, she was feeling light-headed and she loved her husband. What the hell!

She stripped down to her underwear and put on a green skirt and a flimsy top. She did not bother to look at the song sheet: she knew the words backwards. Sheelagh now produced a bottle of champagne and poured them each rather full glasses. Sarah downed the bubbles and felt a warmth inside her. 'Let battle commence,' she said to herself.

The three women climbed down the stairs and re-entered the lounge. They discovered that the five men had created an amphitheatre with carefully positioned lights illuminating the centre stage. The Girls Aloud impersonation group took up their positions with spoof microphones in one hand and initially holding the fingers of another member of the group. The music started and immediately Sarah was leading the performance. She slowly allowed her legs to slide down whereupon her skirt rose up to cover very little.

'*Disco dancing with the lights down low*
Beats are pumping on the stereo.'

She began to feel rather turned on.

'*Neighbours banging on the bedroom wall*
Your sayin' crank the bass
I gotta get some more.'

She was aware that the other two singers were each facing outwards but Sarah was on a mission. She undid the top button of her blouse. The revolving red light caught her in full pose. There were some intakes of breath.

'*Waters runnin' in the wrong direction.*'

For some illogical reason, Sarah thought that the rhyming word should be 'erection' but managed to get back on track.

'*Got a feelin' it's a mixed up sign*
I can see it in my own reflection.'

She stretched upwards as she sang out more stanzas.

'*Somethin' funny's goin' on inside my mind*
Don't know what it's pushin' me higher
It's the static from the floor below
Then it drops and catches like a fire
It's a sound I, it's a sound I know.'

She was now hypnotised by the atmosphere and absorbed in the whole experience. She wondered if she might generate an orgasm. Her skin was sweating and she now found that Sheelagh and Lucinda had linked up with her. They circled round as they sang the third verse and climaxed on.

'It's the sound of the under
Sound of the underground.'

At this point, DC Rudd realised that neither of the two other singers were using the song sheets. It dawned on her that this had been a set-up. She broke away and undid another button on her top: one to go. She stretched upwards and then down she went throwing out in front of her, ankles, shins and thighs. She reached to her waist and removed her skirt. Verses four and five came and went and she became aware that the other two members were tiring and becoming slower in their movements. Sarah released the final button and the material flopped around her arms. She was now singing solo. She softened up her audience with verse six and turned round with her fingers down the top of her knickers. She pretended to push downwards but held the material in place. The five men were utterly absorbed by her performance. Sarah carried on singing.

'And then it drops and catches like fire
It's a sound I, it's a sound I
It's a sound I, it's a sound I know.'

She knew she was tiring but there were many more lines to sing. Sheelagh was holding the microphone to her mouth and going through the motions. Lucinda seemed to have become absorbed by her husband and was standing in front of him. Sarah took centre stage and stood erect. More words followed.

'*It's the sound of the underground*
The beat of the drum goes round and round
In to the overflow
Where the girls get down to the sound of the radio
Out to the electric night.'

Some more lines and then it was over. She had reached the end.

'*It's the sound of the under*
Sound of the underground.'

Sarah rushed from the room and climbed the stairs. She grabbed her clothing and turned to face Sheelagh who was behind her. She took her by the shoulders.

'Go and get your daughter out of my house,' she said, calmly.

She returned down the stairs, found her mackintosh, went over to Gavin Eastman and slapped him across the face. She hauled her husband off the sofa and, holding on to the lapels of his jacket, she ignored his coat and dragged him out of the house. As they reached their front door, Sheelagh was hurrying Lauren down the path: not a word was spoken.

Nick and Sarah shut the door behind them and Sarah rushed upstairs to check Marcus, who was sleeping peacefully. She was joined by Nick. She pulled him into their bedroom, switched off all but the wall light, threw him on the bed, tore off his clothes, stripped off until she was naked, climbed on top of him, hit him with her open hand and then went down on his manhood. In the next forty- five minutes, Sarah and Nick Rudd made love like never before.

'It's the sound of the under
Sound of the underground.'

***

DS Trimble gave DC Sarah Rudd a welcoming smile.

'Good weekend, Sarah?' he asked.

'Pretty quiet, Sarge,' she answered.

'Spit it out. You want to say something, DC Rudd.'

Sarah swallowed. 'It's more what I don't want to say, Sarge.'

'Sarah. It's Monday morning. Get on with it.'

'I want you to trust me, Sarge.'

DS Trimble put down the email he was reading and looked at his colleague. 'Serious?'

'Will you trust me?'

'Let's try, shall we, Sarah?'

'The briefing we had two weeks ago from the Head of Hertfordshire Social Services. They were investigating trafficking in orphans. They suspected a ring because there were some unregistered children appearing. Further there were several where it's thought that the infants might have been kidnapped. He showed us a video of some parents appealing for the return of their children.'

'You have other duties this week, Sarah. We have formed a special public protection team. The Chief Constable is worried both for the children and parents and, frankly, the adverse publicity.'

Sarah handed him a piece of paper. He began to read out the details it contained.

'Doctors Alan and Lucinda Brown. Maplecroft surgery. Gower Street.'

He paused.

'That's just near to here.' He looked at Sarah.

'I need to know your source, Sarah.'

'No, you don't, Sarge. You just have to trust me.'

Late on Monday afternoon, magistrates gave the county police permission to take seven children into care. Nine weeks later, two were returned to their rightful parents in Zimbabwe. The British Medical Association became involved and, despite a lack of evidence to allow the police to prosecute, two doctors were struck off for misconduct and later emigrated to New Zealand.

On her return home that evening, Sarah noticed that a 'For Sale' board had appeared outside the Eastman's house.

As Nick greeted her in the hallway, Sarah put her fingers over his lips.

'You don't ask,' she said, 'and we never talk about it, Nick.'

As her head sunk into the pillow later that night, Sarah mused over a conversation she had overheard in the staff canteen. Another police officer's marriage had hit the rocks: an affair, two more children facing a single parent future and probable financial stress. She was reflecting on a comment made by a police officer from Traffic division.

'They never learn,' he said as he stuffed a bacon sandwich into his mouth.'Coppers should marry coppers.' He lifted up the remaining crust. 'They're the only ones that last.' Some brown sauce dribbled down his shirt.

AN ACCIDENT WAITING TO HAPPEN

May 2003

Caroline Barford-Waverley was seriously rich.

A pre-nuptial agreement, a costly and highly personalised divorce from her Tony Blair donor, banker, husband Clifford, no children and glorious curves. She also had some blemishes on her face: some called them laughter lines.

She slowed down as she joined the A1(M) at junction 5. Soon she would be speeding north towards Peterborough and her anticipated weekend of passion with Balmer. She was driving a BMW something. She didn't really care. They'd owned five cars and she took two of them. She would miss Cliff and he was, eventually, reasonable about her multi-million pound payout. It was his decision to fuck his Director of Human Resources and it was bad luck when their Sunday evening plane back from Nice, after a weekend 'conference', was diverted to Manchester because of fog over Eastern England. Early on the Monday morning, his office had telephoned the home number to ask where they were.

She was looking forward to life after Cliff. She wanted children, which he had refused, and there was plenty of time left. At thirty-one years of age, she could have a football team. It would not be with Balmer because of his Asian background, not to mention his wife and children, but he certainly knew how to treat her, both in and out of bed. She had already secured a job in recruitment in the City, where her contacts were worth a fortune. She'd be starting work on Monday and had given herself six months to find Mr Right No 2.

The facial lines worried her but she felt reassured by the comforting words of the cosmetic surgeon she had seen at his private clinic outside Welwyn Garden City. She flatly refused to allow him to call it a facelift. That was for second division American starlets. They had agreed that she would undergo facial therapy.

She managed to join the Friday night traffic at around five-forty. All three lanes were congested and the rain started at around six-ten. She had the music blaring as she listened to the Three Tenors. She was a confident and prolific car driver. She was also tolerant of others. She pulled back into the centre lane to let a boy-racer through on the outside.

She liked Mr Halpin, her surgeon. He had helped a friend, who had recommended him. He was sure that the treatment would work. He was concerned that she had a drooping left eyelid and he was not prepared to operate on that. She rejected his suggestion that she wear glasses. She braked sharply as a Royal Mail lorry pulled out suddenly. She increased the speed of her windscreen wipers as the rain poured down from the leaden skies.

Nobody had ever told her before that she had a drooping eyelid. She checked in her rear view mirror and was horrified to see what he meant. She tried to pull the skin upwards. She was diverted for little more than two and a half seconds.

A car travelling at eighty miles an hour is progressing at 117.3 feet per second. The driver needs, in normal conditions, 481 yards to stop. Caroline Barford-Waverley was never to discover whether the tables are accurate. She looked back from the mirror and stared ahead of her, screamed, and crashed into a Ford Mondeo, the driver of which was trying to avoid a lorry which had braked and pulled out to overtake a rather nervous old aged pensioner driving carefully in the inside lane. Within seconds, over thirty vehicles were involved and this created mayhem on the other side of the A1 as drivers were unable to take their eyes away from the carnage unfolding opposite them. The rain continued unabated.

***

Sarah Rudd noticed that her one-to-ones with DS Simon Trimble were lingering a little longer. He impressed her. He was unemotional and focused. They began to discuss police procedures and agreed on improvements that might be introduced. He was, as her line manager, taking an interest in her progress with the Sergeant's examinations. Two months earlier, Sarah has passed Part One of OSPRE ('Objective Structured Performance Related Examination') and would soon be facing Part Two which would involve a series of role playing situations.

'I'm supposed to assess your aptitude for promotion,' he laughed. 'But you, Sarah, are a natural. You'll carry rank professionally.'

'I'll carry the pay packet just as well, Sarge.'

'Yes, it's around £6,000 more, I guess.'

'And the rest. I calculate it to be £7,122 which will increase my take home pay by over £420 per month.'

Sarah smiled. 'And that's a lot of money, especially if I avoid getting pregnant.'

DS Trimble looked across his desk and smiled. He looked at his watch.

'Friday traffic. Time for a coffee then we should go home.'

Sarah stood up. 'I know my place, Sarge. Coffee, milk, no sugar. Right?'

He was reading a file when she returned with two mugs, one of which she put in front of him. Purely accidentally, her left shoulder rubbed against the side of his face. Their eyes met.

'I think we're off duty, Sarah. No need for the 'Sarge'.'

'It makes you seem cuddly,' laughed Sarah.

He tasted his coffee and placed the mug down on the desk.

'Don't take this personally, Sarah, but how about a drink at the Moon and Cow?'

'One junction off the A1(M) Sarge... Simon. I'll follow you up there.' She smiled. 'Nice idea. Then home to the welcoming arms of our families.'

Even as they joined the motorway in convoy, they realised there were problems in front of them. There were blue flashing lights and police cars using the hard shoulder. They reached the rear of the incident area and DS Trimble moved over to the hard shoulder until they were blocked by a motorist who had stopped to make a mobile phone call. A traffic patrol was behind them and DS Trimble leaped out of his car.

'Arrest him now,' he shouted at the officers who had arrived. 'Get his car out of the way and then make sure the lane is clear of all vehicles.' He rejoined his vehicle and he and Sarah moved their cars back onto the inside lane where they stopped. They had reached the start of the burning wreckage. There were blue lights everywhere. A fire tender had stopped and the firemen were tackling a blazing lorry. The rain had now reduced to a drizzle. There was a police helicopter hovering over the scene.

They walked for a further thirty-seven yards when they were unable to go any further. A car transporter had swerved and its rear section was overhanging the embankment. Sarah lost sight of her boss as she looked around at the carnage. She then, above the cacophony of sounds, heard a moaning wail.

She ran over into the central area and saw a victim, crushed amongst mangled car parts, crying out for help. She looked around but there was no-one in view. She squeezed through a gap in the metal and managed to get near to the woman's head. She was conscious. There was a small amount of blood coming out of her mouth. Sarah immediately realised that across her chest was a length of black painted car part.

'I'm Sarah,' she said. 'Can you hear me?'

The woman groaned and found a hand which she used to point down at her chest. She made a gurgling noise. Sarah looked around again and shouted out for help. She managed to push her own legs down into a space and get her arms underneath the metal piece across the accident victim. She used all her strength to try to lift the weight: there was a slight movement.

'Thank Christ,' said the woman as she held on.

'Can you breathe better now?' asked Sarah.

'I can breathe,' gasped the woman.

'Can you feel your legs?' asked Sarah.

'No.'

Sarah moved around and tried to locate something she could use to hold the metal bar off the chest of the woman. A fireman arrived and quickly assessed the situation.

'I'll get someone over to you. Hang on.'

Sarah's own muscles were now hurting. She moved around so that she was actually pushing upwards.

'You said Sarah,' groaned the woman.

'Yes. I'm a detective with the Hertfordshire Police. We were on the road.'

'Caroline.' She moaned and spat out some blood. 'Tell me, is my face damaged?'

There was a gash down the one side and some metal splinters through her cheek.

'You look lovely,' said Sarah. She looked around and shouted out. Where was that fireman? She moved her legs and twisted her upper body to try to exert a continuing upwards pressure on the metal block. She had a pain underneath her left arm. She worked out what it was.

'Please don't drop the metal on me,' pleaded Caroline. 'I thought that I was going to die.'

The rain had started up again and there was an eerie silence which was illuminated by a cascade of blue pulsating lights. The only sound to be heard was Sarah's laboured breathing as she was being made to work harder to hold up the weight threatening Caroline's chest. She was in pain underneath her left arm. The flashy area was being painfully pinched. She felt her calf muscle cramping.

She heard a shout and realised that DS Trimble had found her.

'Total chaos,' he said.

'Sarge. I can't keep this up too much longer,' said Sarah.

He assessed the situation. There was no space besides her and although he could get his arms underneath the metal, he was unable to exert an upwards pressure.

'Sarge. Can I ask a favour?'

'What, Sarah?'

'Can you undo my bra?'

DS Trimble gasped. 'Pardon?'

'The strap is twisted under my arm and it's hurting me rather a lot.'

He put his hand underneath her jacket and reached down to her waist. He found her shirt and pulled it upwards. He then located bare skin and moved his hand upwards towards her shoulder blades.

'You're not too good on the geography, Sarge,' laughed Sarah. 'You're heading for my breast. Bit to the left will help.'

Her skin was warm. He travelled as instructed and found the clasp.

'It should just open if you press it, Sarge.'

But nothing happened.

'It's a flicking movement, Sarge.'

'I need two hands,' he said.

'No, you don't. Put your fingers on the top and bottom and twist.'

Suddenly, the bra opened and Sarah's pain under her arm disappeared.

'What a relief. Thanks, Sarge.'

'I've told you. Drop the Sarge, Sarah. Simon will do.'

Sarah looked at Caroline and noticed that her skin

was turning blue.

'Sarge. I've let the metal drop back on her. Quickly, we need to get it off her.'

They worked together. They found that if he put his hands underneath Sarah's armpits, they could raise the obstruction by an inch. The fireman returned and told them that the lifting equipment was on its way. At this moment, a paramedic arrived and put an oxygen mask over Caroline's face.

Fifteen minutes later, Caroline Barford-Waverley was taken by ambulance to hospital. She would later be transferred to a specialist unit for plastic surgery. She was never to reach Balmer and her return to work was delayed by six months.

Sarah and Simon watched the ambulance pull away and moved to the side of the motorway where someone handed them both cups of coffee. Simon then found that he had lost his radio. He put his arm around Sarah and asked her if she would like him to do up her bra. Suddenly, they had their arms around each other and he kissed her. She held on and pressed her body into him. They walked back to his car and got in. They drove up the emergency lane and reached the motorway services. While on their way to the car park, they passed the motel rooms. Nothing was said. Simon parked and went in to book a room. A few minutes later, they were together underneath the shower. He gasped as he held her body.

The next morning, Sarah got up and ordered a taxi. As DS Trimble opened his eyes, she looked down at him.

'This never happened,' she said as she left the room. She had yet to convince her husband why she was late back. He had texted to say he was watching the news pictures on the television. He was asleep when the taxi dropped her off at her home. Her relationship with Simon Trimble regained its previous professional status and neither party mentioned the episode. The incident was closed.

***

Three weeks later, Sarah Rudd realised that her period was overdue. She bought a testing kit and watched the colour appear.

'What do I do?' asked Sarah.

Dr Gerald Taylor gazed at DC Rudd. He had let her talk for over fifteen minutes as she recounted the events at the motorway accident and the irrational rush to bed with DS Trimble.

'This is most unusual,' he said. 'I thought that you asked to see me on a police matter. You were certainly the most interested member of your group when we discussed drink. You need to see your own doctor.'

'I don't need medical advice, Dr Taylor. You're street-wise. As it happens your advice on alcohol led to a battered woman being rescued.'

'Tell me more,' he said.

'No. That's police business. I'm pregnant and I don't know who the father is.'

'You were with this fellow officer just once, DC Rudd?'

'Yes.'

'And you had unprotected sex.'

'Yes.'

'And the test was positive three weeks later.'

'Yes.'

'And you're having regular sex with your husband?'

'Well. Not as often as before but we are together.'

'Before what?'

'I need to know who the father is,' said Sarah.

'Simple. Your husband should take a blood test,' said Dr Taylor.

'Great. Thanks. Hello darling. I've been fucking a fellow police officer. Pop down to the surgery and take a blood test in case you are the father. That's a sweetie.'

'Your husband is almost certainly the father,' suggested Dr. Taylor.

'Is there any way...?'

'No, DC Rudd, and you know that.'

'Fuck.'

Dr Taylor coughed. 'Do you remember when you attended the alcohol session here?'

'Yes. You were impressive, Dr Taylor. I learnt a lot from you.'

'What was my second sign of an alcoholic?'

'What's that to do with my issue?' snapped Sarah.

'What was it, DC Rudd?'

'Alcoholics lie to themselves.'

'Yes. That is what you are doing.'

'I'm pregnant. I'm hiding nothing.'

'Sarah. Do you feel guilty?'

'We should have used a condom. I wanted to but we'd not got the right money for the machine.'

'You shouldn't have been there in the first place. You should have gone home.'

Sarah angered. 'I held that bloody metal off her for nearly forty-five minutes, Dr Taylor,' she shouted.

'And that justified everything?'

'Once. Fucking once. Nick had fancied that sodding Australian...'

'So it was revenge, was it, Sarah?'

'It seemed like a good idea at the time,' she said.

***

The doctor kept them waiting for over half an hour. However, it proved a worthwhile delay as they heard the news they wanted to learn.

As they walked home, Nick put his arm around his wife.

'Will you tell DS Trimble?' he asked. She had told him the whole story. She knew there would be rows and floods of anger but somehow they had talked it through.

'It's nothing to do with him. Anyway, he's on a course. The rumour mill is saying he's about to be promoted.'

'He's a good police officer, is he?'

'One of the best,' said Sarah.

'I have to ask you something, Sarah.'

She knew that this was coming. She had been trying to find the right words in anticipation of his question.

'Did you enjoy it?'

'With DS Trimble, you mean, Nick?'

'Yes.'

She paused and looked at her feet.

'Dr Taylor told me something else,' she said. 'He suggested that stress can be an aphrodisiac. It's not unusual for male patients to get the wrong idea with female doctors. The police force is a haven for affairs because of the situations we find ourselves in.'

'An accident waiting to happen, you might say.'

'I let myself down and I let you and Marcus down,' said Sarah.

'And our new baby?'

'Yes.'

'Perhaps you should understand one thing, Sarah,' suggested her husband.

'Try me,' she said.

'What Dr Taylor said... about stress being an aphrodisiac.'

'That's what he told me.'

Nick put his hangdog look on.

'I've had a terribly pressured time at school today,' he said, looking crestfallen.

'If you don't improve your sense of humour an accident is most certainly going to happen,' she said happily as she hugged him.

The End

Look out for more City adventures featuring Sarah Rudd and her special brand of policing.

If you would like to be notified when the next book is released, be sure to sign up for my free newsletter at:

tonydruryemailsign-up.gr8.com

THANK YOU!

To my Reader:

Many thanks for buying and reading the *On Scene and Dealing: the early career of DCI Sarah Rudd* short stories. I hope you enjoyed reading these insights into Sarah Rudd's career.

If you did enjoy, please post a review on your favourite social media site and let your friends know about *On Scene and Dealing: the early career of DCI Sarah Rudd*.

I hope that this has whetted your appetite to read the novels in the Sarah Rudd City thriller series. You can find details of these in the next few pages.

And don't forget to sign up for my newsletter for details of my latest books and a FREE short story!

tonydruryemailsign-up.gr8.com

Happy Reading!
All the best
Tony

ALSO BY TONY DRURY

Sarah Rudd City Thriller series

Megan's Game: getBook.at/Megan

The Deal: getBook.at/Deal

Cholesterol: getBook.at/TDCholesterol

A Flash of Lightning: getBook.at/Lightning

The Lady Who Turned getBook.at/TheLady

Stories written for HEART UK – The Cholesterol Charity. (All publisher's profits are paid to the charity)

Hannah's Choice

Joanna's Choice: getBook.at/JoannasChoice

Mark's Choice: getBook.at/MarksChoice

The Dinner Party

ABOUT TONY DRURY

Tony Drury is the author of five fictional novels: *'Megan's Game'*, *'The Deal'*, *'Cholesterol'*, *'A Flash of Lightning'* and most recently *'The Lady Who Turned'*.

His main character is Detective Chief Inspector Sarah Rudd. Her early career is told in *'On Scene and Dealing: the early career of DCI Sarah Rudd'*.

He is a corporate financier working in London, Hong Kong and China. He has been described by the financial newspaper *'City AM'* as 'the City's most prolific author.

His first book *'Megan's Game'* is to be made into a film starring Lauren Maddox as Megan. It is hoped to start filming later this year. The film script for '*A Flash of Lightning*' is also being prepared.

Tony is an ambassador for 'HEART UK – The Cholesterol Charity'. He writes short stories ('*Hannah's Choice*', '*Joanna's Choice*', '*The Dinner Party*') with all the publisher's profits benefitting the charity.

Connect with Tony online:
(e) tony@cityfiction.co.uk
(w) tonydrury.com
Twitter: mrtonydrury
Facebook: facebook.com/tony.drury.author
Goodreads: goodreads.com/TonyDrury